DELIVERED
FROM THE
DARKNESS

Delivered from the Darkness
Copyright © 2025
Joseph Monteleone

Paperback ISBN: 978-1-967649-33-4
Hardback ISBN: 978-1-967649-31-0

Published by WordCrafts Press
Cody, Wyoming 82414
www.wordcrafts.net

DELIVERED
FROM THE
DARKNESS

CENT'ANNI
(book two)

JOEY MONTELEONE

WordCrafts Press

Foreword

Good authors are great storytellers. They make the process of producing the worlds create appear simple, the characters intimately close and the events experienced by them emotionally tied to the reader.

Mr. Monteleone is a good Author; he checks all the boxes with his second volume of *Secret of The Storms, Delivered from the Darkness*. It is an epic work completing the saga of the "LeoMorte" family's early 1900s immigration from a small village in Italy to the American dreamland they'd heard so much about as children.

Settling in St. Louis, the Patriarch of the family rises from the poverty of his new Little Italy to become a highly respected member of the city at large. Fighting through what the family believes to be a hundred-year curse, "Big Tony" LeoMorte emphasizes family unity and loyalty as the only way to ensure survival and guarantee success in this new and foreign land. He sees local rules, customs, and even the laws as mere suggestions—a philosophy that enables him to assemble and organize a tightly controlled group of like-minded compatriots.

Delivered from the Darkness stands on its own as the caliber story one learns to expect from Mr. Monteleone's work but we highly recommend it's companion predecessor, (*Cent Anni*) for the full experience of this journey.

Though subtle, the juxtaposition of light and darkness permeate this volume! Philosophically, darkness and light embody opposing yet interdependent forces, each having influence on the experiences and lives of the players in the novel. Light often symbolizes knowledge, clarity, and truth. It reveals what's hidden, dispels fear and offers guidance. Darkness, conversely, represents mystery, the unknown. In *Secret of the Storms* Mr. Monteleone uses both as complimentary forces, for without darkness light loses its meaning, for without light darkness loses its form. As an avid reader, I personally enjoyed the symbolism. Much of the light in *Darkness* is reflective of Judean/Christian values veiling scriptural references commonly familiar to his readers

Whenever a writer reviews a work, he rarely if ever highlights a particular passage or chapter in the foreword. Come to think of it, he doesn't think he ever has ever seen anyone else do it either! It may be improper, but he doesn't care. Remember, in the beginning of this foreword we mentioned how easy Mr. Monteleone made the writing process appear? He does, but it is not. It is incredibly difficult. Chapter Thirteen of *Darkness* is classically illustrative of this. All authors worth their salt mature over time and quantity of production, and that chapter reflects such maturation and effort.

When Mr. Monteleone saw the words "The End" in his mind or put them to paper he knew, as most of us do, that is not the end at all, but the beginning of an immense volume of work that lie ahead.

The combined word count for these two volumes totals approximately 120,000 words. The average manuscript requires five or six rewrites before it is even shipped off to the editors. The maturity of literary talent obviously presented in *Secret* reflects the most likely result of writing and rewriting approximately 828,000 words! Writing such an exquisite tale is a gift to his readers. Another valuable component to the production of such a saga is an often-overlooked ingredient that we know the author would not want overlooked; his wife, companion, inspiration, and critic, in the best sense of the word, Debbie Monteleone!

Thank you, Mr. Monteleone!

~Michael J. Vines

Chapter 1

Life Goes On

Does the sadness ever end? I stood by my father Big Tony LeoMorte's grave: "I know you're at peace now Dad, lying next to mama Maria."

We had buried most of their ashes side by side—unconventional but it was done at their requests.

I thought I was prepared for this, but I soon realized I wasn't.

"It was almost like I breathed your last breath with you, but the moment your worst pain ended, mine had just begun. I felt most loved by Mom but protected from the world by you. I remember things like the smell of Sulphur when you lit a match to fire up your Lucky Strike cigarettes, how you would stare out the window and watch the road in front of the house, how your rough hands turned gentle when holding Mom, how you looked when telling us of the people in your life and stories that had us straining to hear every detail.I watched as the strongest, toughest man I ever knew was betrayed by his body and became fragile yet still proud. God how I miss you. Your headstone reads, *Anthony (BIG Tony) LeoMorte born March 31, 1922–Died October 23, 2013,* but I promise you live on in me.

"Thanks for all the life lessons, Dad. I'll carry them with me always. It's not goodbye, just I'll be back soon. Tell Mama I love her. Rest easy now. I've got this."

I could sense the tears trickling down my face—they felt warm against the chill of November.As I stepped away, I heard the sound of a mourning dove. How appropriate.Driving home my mind was flooded with more childhood memories; maybe this was a defense mechanism from the lingering grief of my losses. During my early years I recall many happy times. World War II had been over for a while, the economy was rebounding, it seemed everyone was living well. There were neat rows of houses with manicured yards, a nice car parked in front, always plenty of food on the table , we played outside until dark catching lightning bugs, walking around using flashlights to light our way in the darkness, and there was fun available for almost those everyone living in the United States. Patriotism was at an all-time high, parades with the American flag prominently displayed, life was simple, school through the week, church on Sunday. On TV, the mornings started with the national anthem, then there was local news, later there were baseball games, family shows and a sign off at midnight. Our lives were like a reflection of a Norman Rockwell painting.

My father often spoke of the sacrifices his parents made when they were immigrating to the United States. During family meals often Dad would recount the details near and dear to his heart.

"Your grandfather left Italy because he was being harassed by the local mafia. He refused to pay them protection money."

My mother chimed in, "People had it rough and wanted to escape to have a chance to live the American Dream that they had heard about."

"When Grandpa and Grandma came over there was confusion about our name. While being processed through Ellis Island the clerk, due to the distractions and noise, mistakenly heard LeoMorte instead to DeoMonte, so he wrote it down incorrectly but then that became our legal name."

I was shocked to learn this bit of family history. "Gee Dad, does that mean LeoMorte isn't our real name?"

"No, that's exactly why it's our legal name, not the original but the legal."

"Boy, sounds like they sure had it rough!"

"Rough, you can't begin to imagine. They came on a train to St. Louis knowing nobody. They could get a fresh start and hide away from the people who threatened them." His tone was serious.

Mama added, "I hope you kids always honor the sacrifice they made."

"Your grandparents and your mother's grandparents made it possible for us to live the lives we're living. Them and a man named Tommy Russo, was a sort of mentor who helped me get started and taught me a lot of lessons."

Too young to work at the restaurant, I picked up work doing anything that would help me prove to my father that I wasn't lazy. I also felt subconsciously the work ethic I have I inherited from Grandpa Vincent and my father. During the harsh Missouri winters, if we got a big snow, when I was off school, I could make money shoveling the snow off the neighborhood driveways. I had another way to earn some cash—the local country club, Sunset Hills, always needed golf caddies, and I got along well with the rich clientele, making two dollars for 18 holes of carrying their golf clubs and normally a tip of another 50 cents. One of the most valuable lessons I learned was to hold on to my money. While the older kids spent every dime, I would hitchhike to and from the golf course rather than pay 35 cents to ride the bus. Another example of my miserly ways was to wait until I got home to eat instead of buying even the smallest item from the vending machines in the caddy shack.

It seemed the curse that plagued the LeoMorte family was over, or was it? The curse was explained to me by Grandpa Vincent years previously when I was just a boy.

While living in Italy, Grandpa had a dream, he says he sees himself walking the edge of the mountains. Moving quietly, he spots a lion in a small opening in the trees and draws back a bow firing an arrow that strikes the lion. The beast falls writhing, thrashing, snarling, and biting at the arrow in its side, blood spurting freely from the gaping wound. As Grandpa Vincent cautiously approaches the lion's breathing becomes labored, and it's clear the massive creature is mortally wounded. He kneels alongside the lion, and as if from nowhere, a deep, raspy human voice intones, "Because of what you've done, your family will experience love and loss, happiness and heartache, and unimaginable agony."

Paralyzed by the ominous prediction Grandpa Vincent can only think to ask, "For how long?"

The lion gasps its final labored breath and utters, "For one hundred years. *Cente'Anni*!"

What an ominous dream!

Late in life, exactly 100 years later I truly believed this family had been unburdened of that terrible curse. I remember the moment well. I looked out the rear window of what used to be my father's home office. I spent time in there mostly because it brought back a connection to my father.

When I roamed the house and especially in his office, I could feel my father's presence and a sense of relief. I walked slowly toward a wooden memorial box made from my grandfather's bread baking paddle, ran my hand over the carved image of the lion's head, opened the lid, and peered at the contents for what must have been a full minute, ashes from my father, his treasured lion's head ring, some of my mother's ashes, and the rosary my grandmother brought with her across the ocean from *the old country*, Grandpa Vincent's wedding band, a dried flower, and a red rose. It seemed I knew what my father was telling me.

The tightening in my throat was a precursor to the tears now dripping from my eyes, I slowly slid the lion's head ring from my finger and laid it in the box, now resting near family remains. As I turned away, a feeling of peace like I had never known swept over me. I noticed the desk calendar. It indicated it was August tenth 2021—Cente' Anni, one hundred years.

At times it seemed escape from the curse was merely fleeting, gone but back again, always looming over us, somehow when least expected constantly returning; just in another form.

Very near the end of his life I remember my father promising me that even after he was gone, he would still be watching over me.

"I'll be there—you won't see me but just know there will be signs that I'm with you."

"How will I know Pop?"

"You'll know."

He was right, there were birds flying and landing close by, someone in a crowd with a cough that sounded just like his, men using his words and even others that looked like him.

I most often felt his presence when I would see something like a stream of natural sunlight breaking through the clouds. It could be the sun peering through the trees, sunrises, sunsets, and occasionally he would make his presence known by sunlight beaming through a small prism we had hanging in the kitchen window. A rainbow of colors streaming from the prism reminded me again of God's promise. In many instances I felt like I could hear his words, sayings that he had that meant very little to me for years now echoed in my head.

I learned to look at the faces of other people when my father, Big Tony, was in a room. I don't think he ever "played the game with sweaty palms." He had quick reflexes, was deliberate in his answers, and different than many of the people who surrounded him—you should be most frightened when he spoke in low, almost inaudible, tones. During the evening after meal time he would sometimes have a cigarette lit, a cup of coffee in his other hand, and go into this straight-ahead stare. He looked for all the world to be deep in thought, totally immersed in something. He never spoke during *the stare* or even after, but there was definitely something occupying the deepest recesses of his mind.

Catherine and I went about our life. There were so many happy times as we made road trips, most close to home, discovering new stores, restaurants, nature and still learning more about each other. Visits from kids, grandkids, and a few friends were welcomed and kept us entertained.

When I was coming in from the outside or in the evening, I would almost always ask Catherine, "So, how was your day?"

"It was fine."

"No really, how was it?" I asked in a sincere tone.

The demise of so many relationships is the slow death of familiarity and diminished genuine communication. I'd seen it in my own family, certainly in my first marriage and in the world round me.

After a while I'd get a more in-depth response from Catherine, "I spent part of my day outside playing in my flowers; wrote out a list of things to do this week and a meal menu. You know how I like to be organized."

"I do. It's one of the things I love about you."

"What else do you love about me?"

Uh oh, now I've opened the door, I realized silently.

"I love the way you take care of me, the house and the effort you put into everything you do."

"What else?" she continued.

"How kind you are to others, you're a good listener and a person of your word. All of those things are important to me... and children, the way you love children."

Her son, Oliver, his wife, Amber, and the grandchildren were always welcome. Holidays were especially cherished, with a tradition of too much food, gifts that had been purchased throughout the year with the comment, "Oh they'd love this," and other gifts went into the closet to be wrapped just prior to birthdays, Christmas or other occasions. I was the worst gift picker. An admitted character flaw, I always bought something that I would like. I worked on that and eventually put more thought into what the person receiving the gift would prefer. Another mistake I was guilty of was substituting money instead of time spent. I inherited this mind set form my father.

I also realized my reluctance to accept gifts was a problem. You can't be a good gift giver if you don't have a good gift receiver.

Eventually after his death I realized that my father was the real glue that kept our family together.

My oldest brother Vince had now been dead for years, Mary Rose was busy with her own family and showed little interest in our sibling relationship, and Dominic, old Dom, had all but disappeared. The distance they created seemed odd to me, but I just accepted it. I convinced myself there was no loss there. Often, I think of my father's frequent proclamation, "family is everything." Was what was left of the family falling apart?

Nonetheless, Catherine and I settled into a comfortable married life with few major interruptions. Each day brought a new sense of peace and calm that I hoped would never go away, but then again, life happens.

The big question and my deepest personal struggle for me, would I be an angel, an instrument of peace or a disciple of the devil, the prince of darkness?

Chapter II

Old Skills, New Ambitions

We had lots of time on our hands, we both felt physically well, we had no financial problems and were on the path to rediscover the joys of this chapter of our lives. Catherine loved our house, loved keeping it clean, loved preparing gourmet meals, and she also enjoyed gardening in the form of landscaping out giant yard. While I never communicated this, I was often reminded of visions of my mother, Maria, doing so many of the same things.

Finally, one day in an unbridled fit of appreciation, I blurted out, "I love you so much, you're a carbon copy of my mother."

Her reply, "That's a huge compliment. I know how much you loved her. I want to take care of you all of our days."

"I'll take care of you. I don't want you to be scared or worried about anything."

"Scared of what?" Her eyes widened as the words slowly escaped.

"For the people closest to me I never want them to be frightened, worried or in pain. I feared that for my father. I never wanted him to be afraid or in pain, but he was both in his last days. I never want to see that in you."

"We can't spend our lives and time in fear of what might happen. We're fine and so fortunate," She reassured.

"I know, it's just tough sometimes. I used to say to people I wasn't afraid to die because I believed I was going to heaven. Now I'm afraid to die because I've had my heaven on earth."

I'd just chuckle when people indiscriminately talked about

being blessed. I wanted to say but didn't, "You want to talk about blessed? Let me tell you my story." I realized that life isn't a contest and let people have their own joy.

After all, I had Catherine, I felt good, had money and other streams of regular income. There was still the sting of being betrayed in my first marriage and some ugly incidents in my life, but who doesn't experience that?

Catherine was my touchstone. We loved each other's company, we laughed and loved regularly, things were humming along, and I was optimistic that the curse was behind us.

Later I introduced Catherine to fishing, and she showed a passion unequaled. She genuinely relished the time on the water and trying to fool a few fish. She quickly became a student of the sport and excelled. I had fished in my younger years and like so many people got busy with job, family, and other activities and had migrated towards other interests. I did, however, enjoy the fresh reintroduction to the sport, and we regularly fished together, sometimes just getting lost in the calm created by the gentle flow of the water; it was medicinal. The drives home were most enjoyable as we recounted the days catches.

Our designated fishing truck sported faded red paint, off-road incurred scratches, a deep layer of dirt, a jumble of equipment behind us in the jump seat, and the smell of fishing was magnified by the warmer days. I never washed the fishing truck because I believed the rust was the only thing holding it together.

Already knowing the answer, I'd ask her, "So how many did you catch today?"

She'd look over at me and say, "I caught three, how many did you catch?"

With a laugh I'd respond, "More than you." That eventually changed. We always smiled, laughed, and this aspect of our lives unconsciously created an even stronger bond between us. We'd watch the weather and plan trips on the water. Pre-fishing days were filled with conversations about past catches, what we might land the next day, and a list of artificial lures we might use.

She'd say we're not competing against each other, but I knew bragging rights were all part of the lighthearted teasing that followed each trip. Most important to me, Catherine seemed genuinely happy on or off the water.

Once arriving home, the routine was the same, kick off your shoes at the door, store the rods, she'd wash her hands and then head for the shower to complete the process. I'd root through the refrigerator swigging orange juice from the bottle only to be interrupted. "I hope you're using a glass and not drinking out of the bottle," she'd call out hearing the refrigerator door opening. She knew me so well. I smiled thinking how predictable I was.

Catherine always cooked something, meals were well-prepared with love and then we'd relax flipping through TV channels while looking for something we hadn't already seen.

As the evening wound down, it warmed my heart when she would ask, "Are you ready to go to bed?"

"I am if you promise to keep me warm tonight."

"No promises, you'll warm up quickly on your own."

The close of the day and a quiet house always presented the notion for me to start what I called, "pillow talk."

There were late night conversations about serious subjects or silly things, treasured memories that could go on for hours. I loved it, she hated it.

"Stop talking, it's time to go to sleep."

This just fueled the fire for me to begin a string of nonsense. I knew it was time to stop when I got the *side eye*, a look of disdain that couldn't be easily dismissed.

A simple, "I love you," brought her back to the kind soul she was.

Through the night I'd wake up and just watch her sleep. She was so still as she slept that sometimes I would lay my hand on her chest to make sure she was breathing. Her little body didn't take up much room in the bed. She looked so tired and helpless.

She would stir and ask, "What's wrong?"

"Nothing, I was just checking on you and loving you." I couldn't imagine life without her. I knew why it destroyed Grandpa Vincent to lose Grandma Rosa so early in life. He was probably never the same, and I assumed bitter—proof of this was after she died, he never even considered at another woman.

At times there were moments when I wondered about Dominic, mostly because I didn't trust him. My parents had always seemed concerned because of his lack of interest in school, his constant bullying of anyone he perceived as weaker than him, and his never ending dark side.

Once I overheard a conversation between my mother and father.

"Tony, do you think there's something wrong with our Dominic?"

"He just needs a little more attention and probably a few more whippings than the others," Dad responded.

"No, he seems to have a temper and can be very unkind, sometimes just mean to the other children and others."

"He's being a boy, an Italian boy. He'll straighten up."

Mama still secretly worried about Dominic. She had reasons to worry! Dominic always seemed to be in the center of some sort of trouble. Even when things quieted down, I always had the feeling it was just a matter of time before the next problem would arise. Even in our own family it was Dom who was at the center of turmoil. Home, school, in the street—it was inescapable,.Dominic was always in some sort of self-inflicted jam.

As an adult Mary Rose seemed to live a relatively tame life but was always preoccupied with wanting to appear socially prominent and *upper class*. There was an unrest about what she drove, where she lived, how she dressed, and an overall complex about how she and her family were viewed. Her own description of her life, home, kids, and even the vehicle she drove had to be embellished to provide the illusion that she and her family were at the height of the social spectrum. Exaggerations were so extreme that people actually avoided her.

Then there was Angelina. She was tucked away in the northeast, still a Catholic nun and now teaching inner city children. Communication was infrequent—a birthday card, Christmas card, or the occasional letter. Again, my father's words caused me concern, "Family is everything." I wondered if the seemingly endless disconnect was due to distance or resentment that life went on in spite of her absence?

Eventually, I was called out of business retirement by a large food processing company that had heard about and admired my supply chain skills, they wanted to offer me a consulting job.

In a phone call the CEO, Mr. Tillman, pleaded, "We need your help. We're out of control and losing our rear ends."

"Sorry, I'm retired and never cared for the impersonal cold corporate structure."

"Name your price, Mr. LeoMorte. We're desperate."

I picked up on the panic and utter desperations in his voice.

"Give me a day to think about it. I'll call you back tomorrow before the end of business."

I already had a computer program that I developed for the Little Italy, the successful restaurant owned by my father. I would just assume the same responsibilities at the restaurant, keeping the inventory, purchasing the necessary items, negotiating prices and forecasting usage, these factors were universal and could be applied easily to other businesses.

I called the next day.

"Mr. Tillman, this Tony LeoMorte. I'll accept the consulting position under these terms. I need three thousand dollars a week, minimal travel, and you have to purchase the computer program I developed, and I still own the rights to the program."

"Wow, those are kind of rough terms and a lot of money, we've never done anything like that."

"Well sir, you called me. If you're not interested, we can still part friends."

"No, no, no… we need your help. It's a deal."

"I'll draw up the necessary legal paperwork and be in touch."

This brought in a significant amount of income and kept me mentally nimble. Little did I know one day this would take us international! So, this was good for the brain *and* bank account, but what about the body? I had a genuine concern for my physical well-being.

After seeing a TV commercial for a two-month trial at the Black Dragon Martial Arts Academy and a little investigation as to the school, I wrote a check for ninety-nine dollars, got my uniform (gi) along with a white belt signifying a new student, and began my training officially enrolled in the summer program. Quickly, I realized this was much more than I expected. I set my sights on getting a black belt in karate. The owner of the dojo, Mr. Taylor Williams, was a shrewd businessman and a very talented martial artist. Williams was high energy and very encouraging. Early on I noticed Mr. Williams walked with a little forward lean, to me a sign of someone with purpose and strong intention.

He approached me one day. "Mr. LeoMorte you're doing well, especially for a man in his fifties."

"Thank you, sir. I like the combination of physical activity and the culture along with learning."

"I was told by one of your instructors that you may have the fastest hands in the school, another mentioned your flexibility and the height of your kicks. You're off to great start."

"I have to admit the far Eastern culture has also intrigued me. The virtues of Bushido, The Way of the Warrior, were very much in alignment with my father's beliefs and core values. Honor, respect, integrity, courage, honest, loyalty, and compassion."

We developed a personal relationship to go along with the business association. After years of training Mr. Williams offered me a part time position as an instructor. I was flattered and decided to discuss it with Catherine. I feared another time-consuming responsibility might be frowned upon.

Once I arrived home I explained excitedly, "Tonight Mr. Williams offered me a chance to be a part-time instructor at the karate school."

"Do you think that's something you'd like to do?" Catherine asked.

"I like to believe I have the heart of a teacher, and I'm interested in the idea of the interaction and being able to instruct others also to watch their progress. Giving people confidence and the ability to defend themselves would also be a plus."

"Will it take too much time away from us?" Catherine wondered.

"I'll just work three days a week and only a few hours each of those days."

"If it makes you happy, then it makes me happy."

She encouraged me to take the offer, just another thing that made me love my Catherine was her unending support.

Life was wonderful. Over the years I learned even more martial arts values, one was to stay aware of everything around me. In Japanese and martial arts, it's called, "zanshin." In my previous life it was called survival.

I had a reoccurring childhood memory. I was still a pre-teen and had convinced my father to let me work Friday nights at the restaurant. I discovered a trap door in the floor of a backroom in the restaurant. I couldn't resist investigating. It was dark, but with a pull on one of the old chains to illuminate the naked light bulb, it produced enough light to provide an ominous view of the strange, dark room below. I descended a ladder leading down, there was a large area with an old wooden table and three chairs. Adding to eerie atmosphere was evidence of paper money, large denominations, some empty wine bottles, and what appeared to be a large blood stain on the floor. What was this place?

After emerging from the secret room, I sought out my father and innocently asked, "I found a really spooky room under a trap door in the floor leading to a basement. What is it?"

The response was something I wasn't prepared for. "None of your business, don't ever go down there again and say nothing to anyone. Anyone, ever!" His tone assured me that this place was off limits.

I knew enough not to ask why.

This and other incidents gave me some insight as to who my father was and how he conducted himself. Without realizing it he possessed the spirit and the values of the Samurai warrior, I never saw him in a situation that he exhibited any kind of fear, always ready and in control.

Most memorable for me were the comments my father made at various times, each a teaching moment. "Listen carefully to what people say when they're mad, you'll know their true feelings," he once said.

Another time he said, "I watch people. I want to know their motivation, which leads to their intent."

"What motivates people?" I asked him.

"Remember this, men are motivated by sex, money, fear, power, ambition, and jealousy. I've learned the problem with money is somebody always wants to take it away from you."

It was confusing to me until I grew older, then it made a lot more sense. He also said, "Look for people's intention. Why do they do what they do? Give your trust begrudgingly and then only to those have earned it, but even then watch everyone closely."

"That seems like a hard life, Dad."

"Life *is* hard, Son. Once you catch anyone in a lie, know this, if they'll lie about small things, they'll lie to you about big things!"

So many life lessons to learn. I came to the realization after a while that you don't have to live it to learn it. Dad's advice was golden.

Chapter III

Is Family Everything?

As a youngster I watched as well as listened closely to my father and his friends. Most were not formally educated people, but they received their advanced degrees in *street wisdom*.

"Being street wise is a survival instinct, and it's what gets you home every night," my father would say. While he never really said it, I knew my family had various levels of trust. Trusting anyone entirely was a risk, and most of the inner circle subscribed to the theory of listen to what they say, but more important watch what they do. A typical Italian trait was to periodically test people, learn their mannerisms, ask them a question you already knew the answer to. If they betray your, trust cross them off the list.

The caution of my father's words echoed in my ears, "If they'll lie to you about little things, they'll lie to you about big things. People lie to cover up, to gain financially, to make themselves look important, and to avoid punishment."

Traditions were a big part of our family life. It started with the naming process. Traditionally each first born boy was named after the grandfather. Conceivably there could be multiple boys with same first name in the immediate families if there were lots of sons. Generation after generation could be traced though ancestral information of where people came from by just the first and last name.

A constant belief held by my parents was the rule that you should be proud of your names.

"What you do outside of this house is a direct reflection on your mother and me."

"Your father is right; people hear our name, and the expectation is that you will conduct yourself like ladies and gentlemen," Mother chimed in.

A caution from my father, "Just remember if you do something outside the house word will get back to us."

"We just want you to be good people, the kind that your father and I can be proud of all the time; people that will be the backbone of our community."

"Your mother is right, what you do at school, in church, or in public is a direct reflect on us, how we raised you," he warned.

The smart move was to sit in silence until *the sermon* was done. Somehow Dominic would always respond with an ill-advised under the breath chuckle, which got the rest of us laughing and warrant the cautionary comment to "knock it off."

A fast fading tradition was speaking strictly Italian. Most immigrants felt the need or were instructed to assimilate to the United States, which required learning English. You could tell when there were *secret* conversations because the discussions reverted back to the familiar Italian to keep the children and non-Italians from knowing what was transpiring.

Churches catered to the ethnic groups in the closest proximity and certainly fell into the tradition category. Families attended services together, supported the church and clergy financially. On Fridays there wasa church sponsored fish fry, usually this was the only time many the Italians didn't eat at home. Midnight mass for Christmas and Easter brought all the congregation, even those who had fallen away from the church.

My father referred to them as "Keysters," those who just showed up at Christmas and Easter.

Meal time, another tradition, centered around family. The days events were discussed, between the parents with the children chiming in when addressed. We all had our specific seat around the table, were expected to be on our best behavior and eat whatever was prepared. Speaking out of turn or unkindly was frowned upon and would generally unleash a comment that was common for those days, by those who clung to the belief that *children should be seen andd not heard*. Harsh but common.

Parents would engage in the how, what, and when questions of each child. "How was school today? What did you learn? When do you get your next report card?"

Short answers like, "Okay," were rewarded with in-depth delving.

"Remember you are representing our family every time you step out that door," my father would remind us.

"Yes, sir," was the only acceptable response.

"Do you understand the sacrifice and suffering grandpa endured to give us all a chance at a better life?"

Stories filled the room. Reactions came in the form of quiet listening from the oldest, Vince, blank stares from Mary Rose, and eye rolls from Dominic. I feared for his safety if my father noticed his insubordination.

Even then I was keenly aware of the people in my life. My father was, sharp in his observations and quick with stern corrections. For transgressions that were deemed unacceptable there was no warning just the sound of his leather belt clearing the loops with lightning speed. That was reserved for us boys.

Mama was a homemaker and a peacemaker. She carried with her that calming effect on everyone, including Dad. For the eldest, Vincent, because he was the namesake of Grandpa, the expectation was he would be the example. For Mary Rose, she was studious and silently resistant to the rules knowing punishment for a girl would be a gentle verbal correction. Dominic seemed unfazed by the threat of *the belt* and was determined to do what he wanted, when he wanted. While I respected my father and mother, there was a high degree of fear in my consciousness. The baby of the family, Angelina could do no wrong, but you dare not question anything she got away with.

Both mother and father frequently showered us with a

measured love and a subtle kindness while maintaining the standard of their own upbringing. The often-heard statement was, "If I had done or said that to your grandfather do you know what would have happened?" There were stories of grandpa's sense of justice. One such tale was the time grandpa caught my father smoking those little stinky Italian cigars.

Caught red-handed, Grandpa Vincent asked my father, "Do you like those?'

Not being sure how to answer Dad unknowingly nodded and said, "Yes."

Grandpa's response, "Good, start eating them."

Grandpa Vincent watched as my father, with his collar firmly in the grasp of Grandpa, was ordered to eat the remaining cigars in the box.

Maybe we didn't have it so bad after all.

Grandpa Vincent seldom smiled. I always believed that was a direct result of his own hard childhood, him having to flee the Old Country for fear of the local gangsters and mostly the untimely death of his wife, Rosa, in her mid-thirties. Left with two boys to raise, it was his burden to bear, but he seemingly gave up and just went through the motions for the remainder of his life. Worked baking bread, ride the bus home, sit on the porch, and repeat.

The story, as I was told, about Grandma Rosa would have broken anyone's heart.

They retired for the night, were hand in hand, neither able to sleep. They stared at the ceiling, minds flooded with thoughts of the future, he pulled her in closely, and they drifted off to sleep.

"Truly God is good. I love you," whispered Rosa to the normally stoic Vincent. They drifted off to sleep.

Slowly Vincent was awakened by the stirring of the boys. Normally Rosa would have been up to start breakfast for her family. He thought how the winter stillness created an unnatural quiet. Barely awake Vincent rolled over, and Rosa was still sleeping. The only light in the room emerged from an open crease in the curtains.

She looked peaceful in the pale light and had a faint smile on her face. He reached over to her and touched her hand—it was cold.

In a surge of emotion Vincent leaped from the bed screaming, "Oh my God, No!" He fell to his knees stunned and speechless by the thought that Rosa was dead. His hands shaking, he struggled to get back to his feet and even breathe. He hesitated to reach for her fearing the final confirmation. He instinctively slid his hands under her back and neck trying to raise her, the earlier jolt of adrenaline robbed him of any strength as she fell out of his arms back onto the bed, limp, lifeless.

Thirty-five years old and gone? Instinctively he hoped this was only another bad dream and repeatedly tried to wake her. He gazed at her, she was pale and cold to the touch, she had passed peacefully and quietly in the early morning hours.

Shocked he pushed a wisp of her hair aside.

Speaking only to himself he uttered, "Rosa, you were surely an angel among us. You left me gently, no pain, no suffering, you just flew off to be with your God."

He found himself studying the contours of her face memorizing each feature, he looked at her like he was seeing her for the first time, knowing he was seeing her for what was likely the last time.

The true depth of his love was revealed as for the first time in a long time, Vincent wept. Vincent had heard people speak of a broken heart, now he clearly knew what a broken heart was. Through his tears Vincent hoped Rosa knew how much he loved her and recounted what was his last kiss and his expression of love. He felt the moist warm tears on her face and suddenly thought maybe she was just sleeping, but he realized those were his tears on her face.

He knew the only woman he had ever or would ever love was now gone. Grandpa would never be the same. He sank deeper into a silent shell, rarely speaking, sullen and certainly never given to any laughter. Attempts to start conversations had to be approached cautiously. Starting with the weather was pretty safe.

"Hot out here today, isn't it Grandpa?"

He generally responded in one word like, "Ninety-five."

"Do you have any tomatoes on your plants?"

"A few."

"So, how are you feeling?"

"Okay."

"Alright Grandpa, I'll see you tomorrow, *domani.* (Tomorrow in Italian.) That would coax a smile from him. He appreciated my attempts to speak to him in his native tongue.

After Grandpa Vincent died, we were very surprised to find all the birthday presents as well as any Christmas gift given him over the years tossed into a closet unopened. How incredibly sad.

High profile citizen and mob muscle, Tommy Russo, taking my father under his wing was truly a godsend. Russo, married with no children, was an early day mentor to my father. He treated him as if he were his own son and guided him away from the dark side of the downtown streets, and he eventually willed him the restaurant at a nominal price. Russo without a doubt changed the trajectory of my father's life.

Tommy Russo was as tough as the come but had a blend of compassion to go with his tough as nails persona. Tommy watched out for my father.

Tommy once advised his young friend, Tony, "Remember when I said, nobody will take better care of you than you? Well, I've never been afraid to mix it up when I had to. I don't want to fight, but I will. Do you know the rules of street fighting?"

A timid Tony replied, "I think so."

Russo's response came quickly, "By your answer I'd say no. In fighting *there are no rules.* You always know who the winner is—he's the one still standing. Your enemy won't always come after you, they go after who or what you cherish the most."

My father would never fully understand this until the most unspeakable tragedy hit the LeoMorte family years later.

Chapter IV

Ghosts Resurrected from the Past

If life had taught me anything it was to not get too comfortable, challenges are just around the corner.

Fear can be a terrible thing. At times, even as a youngster, I believed that I saw fear in my mother's eyes. I couldn't imagine what might make her fearful or even uncomfortable. Usually she seemed most frightened when the police would show up at the house. This had become a regular occurrence mainly because of their dislike of my father, his associates, and people like them made the law frequent visitors. It appeared to be a cat and mouse game. They'd show up at all hours, especially one intimidating man, Kevin O'Rourke. Normally there were always at least two at a time. Flashing paperwork they would proceed to do a thorough search of the entire house and grounds.

The common greeting was *Mr. (or Mrs. LeoMorte) we have a search warrant.* After checking their credentials my parents would round us up, take us to the living room as the police searched everywhere.

Once, privately, I asked my mother—I didn't have the nerve to ask my father—"What are the policemen looking for when they come here?"

In a rare moment of weakness my mother my mother explained. "They think we have bad things here."

"Bad things, like what?"

"Guns, drugs, stolen items, large amount of cash, paper money."

"Do we have anything here like that?" I wondered out loud.

She tired of the interrogation. "Enough questions, little Tony."

Her hesitancy to answer gave me even more reason to wonder about her demeanor when questioned about the presence of the law in our lives. Should I ask my father, or would that just make things worse?

There was a distinct darkness about this situation with my mother that was troubling. Mama was normally a happy go lucky kind of person until she went into *that* place. It seemed that she tried to treat each of her children the same, but with Dominic she could become impatient and even looked at him differently. Maybe because he was a problem child—or did she harbor some sort of resentment towards him? He didn't look or act like any of the rest of us. I clung to the idea that eventually time would tell.

As for my father, he was clever and was always way ahead of everyone, or so it seemed. Proof of his genius was one of the things he did when we moved into our big home. While he was remodeling, he had a special request of the contractor.

Tony approached the crew boss, Andy. "Here's a list of inside work, but I also have some outside projects for you. I want you to pour a six-foot by six-foot concrete slab with a four by two hole, dig the hole three feet deep in the center of the slab and then surround the whole thing with a seven foot chain link fence, install a gate to match the ten-foot by ten-foot enclosed fenced area. I also want you to build a doghouse measuring five and a half feet by three feet. Make it sturdy. It's going to be home to a big male German Shepherd."

"Sir, you can buy a doghouse a lot cheaper than if you have me build one."

"Just build it and put it on a set of rails."

"A doghouse on a set of rails?" Handy Andy" asked.

"On a set of rails so I can slide the doghouse back. Do you understand?

"Yes sir, Mr. LeoMorte."

"I have someone who will do you a good job."

"Did I hear you correctly, a doghouse on a set of rails?
"Yes!"

In my father's business, restaurant and otherwise, most of the transactions occurred in cash, lots of cash! Law enforcement would have loved to locate a giant stash of cash for leverage in prosecuting based off income tax purposes and other possible illicit reasons.

On one of the most memorable raids my father turned to the lead agent, a square-jawed, broad-shouldered man who identified himself as Kevin O'Rourke, and in a loud voice proclaimed, "We have a search warrant for your entire home and the adjoining grounds."

Calmly my father asked, "Can I put my dog up? He's a large German Shepherd and doesn't like strangers." It's strictly for the safety of you and your men."

"Go ahead, one of my men will accompany you."

As my father stepped out into the backyard he ordered, "Rocky, get in your house!"

The big guard dog immediately responded by obediently going into the enclosure and laying down. Tony closed the gate to the kennel and motioned for the agent it was now safe to come out.

As soon as the agent stepped into the yard the dog went into full attack mode jumping into the fence and growling his displeasure at the invasion by this intruder. Tony followed the agent around the yard as the FBI men inside went through the house in a room by room search, the dog never stopping its relentless display of anger.

For years after the raids my father wore a smile on his face knowing once again, he had made fools of the law. That concrete enclosure under the dog had a huge amount of cash, bundles neatly wrapped in heavy waterproof plastic. Cleverly concealed under the dog house were millions of dollars.

While my father chuckled after the visits, it seemed to take hours for my mother to calm down. Eventually the immensely dark reason for this would be revealed.

While it appeared the LeoMorte family had dodged the ancient curse, the threat was always lurking just beneath the surface.

Many times, when my mother was out of hearing distance, I'd hear my father either on the phone or in far corner of the house discussing business.

A particularly chilling statemen that I overheard added to the fear I had of the character Big Tony LeoMorte. Apparently enraged with someone, he blurted out to the party on the other end of the phone, "Your enemies are like wine grapes, they're better when they're stomped flat!"

Meticulous about safety precautions he watched out windows for strangers, unfamiliar cars, and even had bodyguards start his car occasionally. Fear can be a motivator or an unwelcome companion.Along with the consistent theme of *family is every-thing* were the measures taken beforehand—preventive measures taken regularly. My father used to say, "I don't like surprises." In our lives there always seemed to be surprises, a few good, some catastrophic.

When things were good, they were almost monotonous. But business activities were consistent and there was evidence that money was rolling in. Normally may parents' room was off limits. I often wondered why. Sometimes we were allowed in, maybe for a last good night kiss or to briefly discuss the next day's events or our parent's expectations. Once I was on one of these rare visits and noticed a gun on the night table on my father's side of the bed. He slept on the side that gave him visual access to the entry. I'm sure this was to protect my mother if there were to be an intruder. Along side the gun on the night stand was a wad of money—a roll of bills wrapped and always topped by a hundred-dollar bill.

On the rare occasion when my father was in public paying for something, it was always with cash. Most regular business owners insisted, "No charge Mr. LeoMorte."

I liked the look on the faces of people when he would *flash the cash*. He'd peel off hundreds, fifties and occasionally smaller bills. Most transactions were punctuated with the phrase, "Keep the change." My parents both had class—my mother in her style of dress, her carefully chosen words, and her ever-present politeness.

With my father, it was his snappy attire, dressed impeccably, his poise, confidence, and ability to control the room anywhere he went. We were dressed stylishly, well-groomed (Mother made sure of that), and were always (well most of the time) on our best behavior. Any transgression or departure from the normal expectations would be met with swift corrections. Usually just *the look* and clearing of the throat was all that was needed. This was especially true in church. The seating arrangement was child, one of the girls, a boy, parent, boy child, parent and another boy child, girl. We still overlapped but we knew we could be reached and a quick pinch of the skin under the arm was all it took to know this was just the warning. The girls were immune from correction, mostly because they behaved, but the LeoMorte boys seemed to be prone to lapses in judgement.

When things got out of hand, and our behavior was questionable, the belt whirled through the loops of Dad's pants. No sense running—that would only make it worse. Crying and pleading for mercy was fruitless. If the belt came off, one or all of us were going to get it. It didn't happen often, and the truth is, had we been caught in all our mischief we would have face the wrath of Dad more frequently. Vincent was expected to supply the example for us younger kids, Mary Rose was a quiet spirit, but the antics of Dominic and Angelina made up for all of us. I reveled in the fact that, compared to Dominic, I was a great kid. Dominic frequently took his resentment out on each of the siblings and even the dogs.

A whirlwind of activity, my childhood was confusing, sometimes scary. Night terrors were common, fear of getting in trouble often kept me from making poor decisions. Later in life I realized I was doing the right things for the wrong reasons.

When things got too hectic, I would isolate myself. I remember once climbing up a tree because the commotion was too much. This practice of isolation would follow me in adulthood. When things were spinning out of control my peace came from getting as far away geographically or mentally as possible. I recognized the need for organization and routine as being my safe place, the modern explanation is called OCD. In my business life, these qualities actually served me well. I strived to develop my own system until I was satisfied that my way or plan was successful and then went into the mode of study, experiment, apply, gauge accomplishment, and repeat. Dull, but it kept me centered and calm. I lived in my own little world.

All in all, as a family we still led a pretty charmed life.

Chapter V

Bunny's Back

Bonnie Dempsey had a significant impact on the LeoMorte family. It started one day at the restaurant, a day that would in many ways alter our family's lives. On a Friday as the lunch crowd was arriving, in walked a group of well-dressed women, all drop dead gorgeous. Big Tony spotted the group and made his way quickly to greet them.

"Hello ladies, I'm Tony LeoMorte."

A few giggled at the thought that someone wouldn't recognize the now famous St. Louis figure.

The lady at the front of the group said in a low sultry voice with a deep Irish brogue, "I'm Bonnie Dempsey."

Tony, trying to turn on the charm asked, "Did you say *Bunny?*"

The amused women laughed in unison.

"*Bonnie.* Bonnie Dempsey," the lady said correcting LeoMorte

Tony was taken by the beauty of each of these women, but especially Bunny.

Along with that accent, she had the most amazing red hair and the greenest eyes he had ever seen. Her figure and her smile all made her look like a woman who would grace the cover of any magazine. He figured her to be about 30 years old.

"Do you ladies work downtown?"

"I run a modeling agency here," Bonnie replied

"First time here to Little Italy, because I can assure you, I would have remembered a woman of your beauty and obvious good taste in choosing to dine with us."

"Yes, my first time, but I'd heard of this place and of course of you, Mr. LeoMorte."

Now they were both blushing after the verbal volley of compliments.

"Let me show you to our best table reserved for the most elite customers."

As he led them to a table, he added, "This table will give you some privacy and yet a great view of downtown." He quickly pulled the chairs out for each of the women, then Tony motioned for a waiter to come over.

"These lovely ladies are my special guests, take good care of them."

"Thank you, sir," Bonnie said flashing that million-dollar smile.

"Tony. It's Tony. Let me know if there's anything you need, anything at all"

As other customers entered, Big Tony gave them standard greetings, but he couldn't take his eyes off the group of women—especially Bunny. He remembered this feeling from when he was a teenager. She returned his glances with a subtle wink, and the 44-year-old man felt butterflies in his stomach, something he hadn't felt for years. He noticed she was wearing a wedding ring, and the realization hit him that he too was married. And Tony really loved his Maria.

Their meal done, the ladies thanked Tony for the great food and excellent service.

"Most of us are from out of town, but when we get to St. Louis we'll be back."

"How about you, Bunny. Are you from out of town?"

"No sir, now I'm a St. Louis girl by way of Dublin, Ireland."

Bunny and her friends came to the restaurant regularly after that. One evening Bunny walked into the restaurant escorted by a man she introduced as her husband, Sean Dempsey. My oldest brother, Vincent, makinge a poor attempt to mimic my father's charm, said "Welcome Bonnie," and then took her hand and kissed it, immediately sending Sean Dempsey into a rage.

As was my father's way, he appeared to smooth this awkward situation over quickly.

"My son Vincent certainly didn't mean any harm or any disrespect. Please allow me to show you to a table."

The glaring Sean Dempsey was escorted and seated at the best table in the house with his wife seated next to him. A peace offering, a bottle of wine, was promptly delivered. Tension remained high but seemingly things had calmed down. My father's eyes never left the couple that evening. While Vincent had made an error in judgement, my father would never allow anyone to harm any of our family.

Big Tony could wear several hats. Despite a limited formal education, he could speak eloquently, was well versed in current affairs, had the right words for any occasion, and had high level connections at his disposal. Below the surface it would be fair to say Tony LeoMorte was rough around the edges.

There were stories that seemed to contradict each other about who this man was. One day while at the restaurant, I was told about a heroin addict that came in asking for a hand out. He talked to the man and realized he knew some of his family, he ushered the man to a back room, fed him, and tucked a twenty-dollar bill into his shirt pocket as he left. On the same day a young thug walked in loudly proclaiming he would fight anybody in the place. Slipping behind the check-out counter, my father emerged with a sawed-off double barrel shotgun and rammed it directly into the tough guy's face promptly breaking his nose. He was last seen spewing blood and making a hasty retreat.

My father and mother had similarities in many ways, and in some others they couldn't have been more different. Maybe that's why they got along so well. While both their lives revolved around family, my mother was kind, trusting, and showed her feeling by taking care of all our basic needs and watching over us like a guardian angel. Tony LeoMorte, my father did the same but in a different way. Firm and vigilant, he felt his actions were proof enough of his love for his family.

One tenet my father lived by was an unwavering belief—"Never reward bad behavior. It's black and white, no grey area, very few second chances, and limited forgiveness."

After Vincent, the next child up was Mary Rose—stoic, rigid, and reserved. Dominic was the wild card. Dom talked a good game but couldn't back it up and leaned heavily on the LeoMorte name and my dad's reputation. I considered myself to be a cross between my parents—sensitive like my mother but explosive when pushed like Big Tony. That left Angelina, who by her own admission was spoiled—Daddy's little Angel.

Mama Maria did have some close friends and made time to socialize, she loved to entertain in our home. It was always immaculate and viewed by visitors as a show place. There were always homemade treats, coffee, tea, and conversation. Gathered around the table, Janice, Ann, and often Stephanie who had earned the nickname, *Feffanie,* because granddaughter, Connie, Mary Rose's child, couldn't pronounce her name.

It was a unique blend of people and personalities. Janice was a retired school teacher who knew everything bout plants and creatures wild and domestic. Janice also was well versed in old school homemaking, canning, and raising her own food—skills seemingly lost to today's world. Ann was involved in the medical field and was the member of the group who stayed current with all thing's computer. She seemed to have a way with children. She was always kind and patient with all of the neighborhood kids. Ann was solid, dependable, and had a contagious laugh. She was always willing to help anyone. Ann could be counted on to show up early, help set up, and stay until the place was cleaned up and every dish done. Stephanie was a gourmet chef. she could make a huge meal or put together a snack tray with equal ease. Everyone loved *Feffanie.* She had a pixie smile, a kind word for everyone, and was famous for her willingness to assist in any community service. Nicole, a single mom whose life centered around her children, rounded out the group. She fit in well with everyone else. She was cute, kind, and rarely missed a get together.

This group was surely something special, and my Mama Maria fit right in. She seemed to have the unique quality of making everyone feel at home and welcome. She was generous with her time and gifts, while also blessed with traditional homemaker's skills.Pleasant afternoons usually ended before spouses, children, or grandchildren arrived. Sometimes Ann would stay around to help clean up against my mother's constant protest.

"Don't be silly, Maria. Many hands make light work," Ann would say amid my mother assurances that, "I can do it." Ann had a few struggles in her early life, married the bad boy who was dragging her and her children down. She talked openly one on one with my mother. I recall one day when my mother sat across from her friend with tears slowly streaming down her face.

"What's wrong, Maria?" wondered Ann.

"Nothing, sometimes I get overwhelmed by things."

"I'm glad to listen if you want to talk it over."

"No, it's something I keep to myself. I just can't talk about it."

"Okay, but you know I'm here if you need me."

They hugged, and Ann left quietly, turning around at the door looking like she had something else to say, but she paused then moved slowly out the front door.

Overhearing this exchange was disturbing to me, but I didn't know how to help with grown-up problems. I seldom saw my mother cry, so this was imprinted in my memory.

I still often looked at her, silently wondering what this trouble could be.

Many years passed, and it was an October afternoon. This was one of my afternoons to teach at the karate school. I've heard people say, "You know you're good at something if you can teach it." I knew there were others with decades of experience, certainly many more years than me, but I worked hard to learn, and just as important I was able to relate to most of the students regardless of age, physical skills, or community position.

I had multiple responsibilities—there were the beginners, the white belt adults, intermediate students, and I assisted in advance class instruction as I earned my black belt second and third degrees. It was always interesting to see the esteem this group had for the black belts and especially the instructors. Intermediate classes were some of my favorites, I encouraged them to stick with it while I tried to make the classes a physical challenge but also fun. I would do all the warm ups and exercises along with them to make them feel closer to me. Many stayed around to watch the upper belts train and spar. Sparring is partially the test of natural skills and application of lessons. At one point I was encouraged by others, so I begrudgingly signed up to compete in a big karate tournament. Over twenty-two states would be represented, and once I came to my senses, I wondered what I had gotten myself into. My fear of failure kicked in as I tightened my black belt around my waist. Running *kata* or forms is a series of choreographed moves to defend and attack if necessary. Somehow I was also convinced to participate in *kumite*—point sparring or fighting. You face new opponents until you lose. First round goes quickly. I win but come out with what turned out to be two cracked ribs from a brutal body kick. Match number two turns out be another win, then three and four, finally a close one, but I win!

The next week it seemed I had earned some additional respect. As I was finishing my six o'clock class, I saw someone approaching from the hallway to the observatory. No, it couldn't be! It was, it was Bonnie Dempsey. Wow!

Who knew years later these circumstances would lead to a reappearance of Bunny. What would it mean? It would change my viewpoint and my life.

Chapter VI

Shadows of Reflection

Up until now it was a typical day at the karate school. I was dressed out in my gi, my black belt tied snuggly around my waist and ready to teach an intermediate adult class. I felt a sense of accomplishment each time I cinched my belt. Priding myself on being aware of my surroundings, this particular day I was taken by surprise. Out of the corner of my eye I saw a figure moving down the narrow hallway coming closer to me with each stride.

A little older but instantly recognizable with her flaming red hair and deep green eyes, she looked pretty, much the same as I remembered her. I was without words.

"Remember me?"

Still in shock, I replied, "Bonnie? Bonnie Dempsey? Is it you?"

"It is."

She leaned in and gave me a gentle kiss on the cheek. I thought it seemed odd and a bit inappropriate, especially in the middle of the karate school and from someone I hadn't seen in years.

"How have you been?" she asked.

Still a little surprised to see her, I replied politely, "Doing well, and yourself?"

"I'm okay."

Now the obvious question. "What are you doing here?"

"My grandson is one of your karate students," she replied.

"Grandson? Who is that?"

"Daniel Dempsey."

"Daniel is your grandson?"

"He is."

Then I nervously made the trite statement, "Well they say it's a small world."

"When he mentioned his karate instructor's name I just knew it had to be you," she said smiling.

"He's a good student and very respectful."

"Is there a place we can talk privately?" she whispered.

"I'm about to teach a class," I replied.

"Well then, would it be possible for us to meet one afternoon?"

"Okay, but why?"

"I just have some information for you."

"Let's see ,today is Wednesday, I don't have anything scheduled tomorrow, is that okay?"

"Sure, that would be great.

"Tomorrow at 10 for coffee at the Union Station Café?" I offered hesitantly.

"I'll be there," she assured me.

As I drove home that evening, I tried to recall the last time I saw *Bunny,* (as my father called her) Dempsey. It had to have been the night she shocked my parents with some incredible revelations that would change all of our lives.

I found myself reliving a life changing memory—Bonnie Dempsey showing up at our house, my father being surprised to see her standing on the hallway. After an awkward introduction, my parents went into our living room, and the conversation between the adults began. Our world would never be the same.

"Mrs. LeoMorte, I'm Bonnie Dempsey. Thanks for seeing me."

"Come on in let's sit down. Can I get you a cup of coffee?" Mama asked.

I recall my mother ushered her into the living room, my father followed close behind.

"Coffee would be great, maybe it would calm my nerves."

Mama Maria left for a moment comes back carrying a tray with coffee, cream, sugar, and a spoon.

"Thank you. Father Parisi had nothing but nice things to say about you, and I can see why," offered the visitor.

"Oh, you knew Father Parisi?" Mama inquired.

"Well, I only saw him three different times, but yes, I knew him. The first time I met him it was just outside the restaurant. He was coming out as I was going in, we introduced ourselves, and I had a conversation with him. I was instantly comfortable with him and asked if I could come to visit him and get some counseling. He agreed, and we set a date for a few weeks out."

My father and mother were listening intently, wondering what could have possibly been the purpose of this very unexpected visit. For one of the few times, I could tell Big Tony was getting nervous. Beads of sweat broke out on his forehead, and he began tapping his foot on the floor. I'm sure he was hoping his heartbeat wasn't audible.

"I have some news for you, I'm afraid it's bad news. I received a box and a letter." Bunny then pulled out a very familiar ring, a lion's head ring. "This was your son Vince's ring."

Big Tony lunged toward her and grabbed the ring from Bunny as Maria gasped and began to look unsteady like she might pass out.

My father demanded in a thunderous voice, "Where did you get this?" He quickly moved to Maria's side to hold her up.

"It came in my mail with a letter." I can read you the letter if you want me to." Without waiting for a response, Bunny unfolded a single sheet of paper, slipped on a pair of glasses and began.

"Here's a souvenir for you, I took it off the finger of your lover, Vince LeoMorte. I wanted to kill his father, but he always had bodyguards around him, so I waited. I waited in the parking lot of their restaurant and grabbed Vince at gun point and forced him into my car and made him drive across the Mississippi river into Illinois. I walked him down to the edge of the river and took his wallet, his watch, and this ring so he couldn't be identified. Then I shot him and dumped his

body into the Mississippi river. It was high and muddy, and I believed that would assure he was never found. Later, I took the diamonds out of the eyes in the ring, sold them, and thought you should have it now. Now he's lost his son like I lost mine. Good-bye Bitch!"

After a long pause Maria in a shaky voice asked, "I don't understand any of this?

Bunny explains, "Sean *wasn't* my son's father. He thought it was Vince or maybe Big Tony."

Maria cast her eyes toward Big Tony, eyes of hurt and doubt. Bunny seeing the disbelief in her eyes asked, "Can I explain please?"

Maria, through tears her voice shaking, said, "Go ahead."

"For nine months I carried a baby *and* a secret."

Maria took on a look that somehow, she understood, a look that conveyed a kinship for the fear, shame, and anguish this woman felt.

"The second time I saw Angelo Parisi was when I went to see Father Parisi as you know him, because I was infatuated with your husband. I was overwhelmed by the feeling that Tony LeoMorte was good looking, rich, and powerful—that's an undeniable aphrodisiac for any woman. I met Father Parisi at the church, we went out into the garden area behind the priest's house, I was starting to talk when it began to rain. We ran into the house to escape the downpour, no one else was there. As I told my secret Father Parisi hugged me to comfort me, an innocent hug and our faces brushed. That turned into an accidental kiss, and then we got carried away. He broke his vow of chastity and me, I broke my marriage vow. I went home immediately ashamed and afraid. I had sex with my husband, Sean, for three days in a row as if it would erase my indiscretion. Years after my son was born it was determined Sean couldn't have been the father."

More tears trickled down the face of Maria, she understood in only the way another woman could of the torment Bonnie had suffered with all the secrecy surrounding the taboo and outcome of her sin.

"The third time I saw Angelo Parisi was the same day my son and I went to see Father Parisi in the hospital. I had heard he wasn't well. I waited for a while with a now grown Mickey in the parking lot unsure of how this might go. When we went to Father Parisi's room, he was barely able to recognize me, and he had never seen Mickey. His illness had caused him to lose a lot of weight, the room was cold, sterile, and wreaked of a combination of antiseptics and sanitizers. I introduced the two, to which Mickey replied, "So, this is your Father Parisi that you always talked about."

"I took a deep breath and said, "No this is *your* father…Father Angelo Parisi."

"They both looked at me in horror.

"Mickey whirled around asking, "Did I hear you right?"

"Father Parisi laid there speechless, tears slowly made their way down is hollow facial features. As he turned toward me, I resisted, looking away in shame. He exhaled loudly, it sounded almost as if he had the wind knocked out of him.

"I explained further, "This is Michael, Mickey I call him. You would be proud of him. He's a good man, kind, gentle, and even got an academic scholarship offer and an athletic scholarship offer to Notre Dame. He was the valedictorian of his class and a high school All American soccer player. He's getting a degree in theology."

"The priest could scarcely lift his hand but reached through the rails of the hospital bed to hold the hand of this child turned man, unbelievably his son. He asked Mickey to lean over and he whispered to him, Mickey shook his head yes as to acknowledge the words the priest, his biological father, whispered. Father Parisi kissed Mickey's hand and pulled it close to his chest.

"I leaned in and said, "I'm sorry I didn't tell you sooner. I let my fear and my conscience stop me, I wanted to tell you hundreds of times. You had a right to know."

"He nodded yes slowly and raised his shaking hand to make a sign of the cross toward me. I took it as an indication that he forgave me and in my mind was granting me absolution.

"Mickey moved to the other side of the hospital bed; his face contorted with emotion. Father Parisi reached for both our hands, placed them together as if to unify us all and then closed his eyes for the last time. His last breath was labored and followed by a small gasp.

"As we left the hospital, I thought, *We were two imperfect people who made a perfect baby that turned into a good man.*"

Bunny continued her story, "The drive home was quiet. I only hoped two things, that my son would understand and also forgive me."

Bunny looked at Maria and spoke, "Directly or indirectly I've brought immeasurable misery to your life. No words can describe my sorrow from one mother to another for what's happened. I'm begging for your forgiveness."

Tony turned to Bunny and asked, "Where did the letter come from?"

She said, "It was post marked, Dublin, Ireland. I'll leave it here if you want me to."

Without another word my father left, climbed the steps to his bedroom, and let out cries of anguish that didn't even sound human. Why had these secrets and this seemingly unavoidable curse followed him?

After an hour downstairs my mother slowly climbed the steps and went to what used to be Vince's room and looked around at his pictures, high school trophies, and the clothes left in his closet so many years ago. Now she could put her son to rest, at least in her head. Gruesome as it was, she now knew what had happened.

Mom found Dad face down on the bed still sobbing. His eyes bloodshot, he was drained physically and emotionally. He had no more tears to shed. They stared at each other, fell into each other's arms as if wondering how they could go on.

I stood undiscovered near their doorway and heard and saw things I wished I never had. What a terrible night! This was one of the memories I wished I could erase.

Now I couldn't help but wonder what in the world could this woman want now? Should I trust anything she said? This whole thing seemed to warn of trouble—trouble I didn't need and didn't want. I'm sure I began to overanalyze all of this. So many questions from wild to tame. What is this really all about? Should I just run, ignore this reemergence of one of the darkest experiences of my life? My stomach was unsettled, pretty sure my blood pressure was elevated, and I realized that my palms were sweating. As I pulled into my driveway, I was wishing the drive had taken longer to allow me more time to sort this out.

I must have been giving visual clues that I was shaken. Catherine took one look and asked, "What's wrong? You look completely stressed."

"Give me a minute please."

"What's wrong? Are you okay?" she pushed further.

"I was just visited by a ghost from the past, the real thing."

"What are you talking about? You're scaring me."

"Don't be alarmed, we're not in any danger, but the woman that was in part responsible for a family tragedy came to see me today."

I told Catherine the details of my clandestine meeting with Bonnie Dempsey. Much like me she was curious about the unexpected return of this woman and why she contacted me. So she wouldn't worry, I told my wife the time and location and all the details of the rendezvous. That night my attempt to rest was troubled to say the least.

Not able to go to sleep I imagined the first time I saw Catherine. It was at a St. Louis symphony performance, and I was only there because a longtime restaurant customer practically forced the tickets on me.

I remember every detail; the conductor addressed the audience with a welcome and the announcement that the opera, *Rigoletto*, was about to begin.

The lights dimmed, and the music started. To my surprise I was actually enjoying it.

After about 45 minutes a voice came over the speakers announcing a brief fifteen-minute intermission, and then it happened. I stood up to stretch and turned back looking into the crowd. About six rows up I spotted the woman of my dreams. She appeared petite, black hair that matched a raven's wing, eyes that looked translucent but were an ice blue, modest make up which didn't disguise her natural beauty. The *wow* button was going off in my brain. I guessed her to be at least 10 years younger than I. I was instantly drawn to her. My mind raced. *Who is she? Is she married? Why is she sitting alone at the St. Louis symphony. I hope she isn't from out of town. I hope she doesn't have a can of mace in her purse,* I thought as I climbed the steps toward her row to introduce myself.

I started a conversation with the dignified look lady next to her in hopes of not scaring off my dream girl.

"Ma'am how would you like to have a second-row center seat? I'm leaving soon anyway."

"Why I would love that, how very kind of you."

"Here you go enjoy. The rest of your evening."

I scooted clumsily out of the way so I could *accidentally* bump into my dream girl. "I'm sorry. I didn't mean to bump into you. Are you okay?"

"Of course, you barely brushed me."

"I'm Tony LeoMorte, it's a pleasure to meet you."

"You really haven't met me yet," she said with a laugh that rivaled the sweet music of the symphony.

Is this lady for real? "Okay, let's formally meet then."

"I'm Catherine, Catherine Collins. What else would you like to know?"

"Since you asked, can I buy you a cup of coffee after the symphony?"

"You want to buy a cup of coffee, huh?"

"What I'd like to buy you is a two-carat perfect princess-cut diamond ring set in platinum, but how about we start with the coffee." That a got a full laugh!

"I can't tonight."

"How about tomorrow?"

"Let's make it Friday. That will give me time to do some research on you," she said playfully.

"Uh-oh. Let me help you—I don't like sushi, long walks on the beach, or Barry Manilow. I'm a Pisces, and I think you're the most beautiful woman I've ever seen."

She quickly responded, "Did I mention Barry Manilow is my brother, I love to eat sushi while I walk on the beach, and by the way your zipper is down."

I panicked but didn't want to look down, so I countered with, "Well they say it pays to advertise."

This woman was beautiful and witty. *Wow!* I couldn't look away; she was about five feet tall, and the combination of black hair and blue eyes gave her that movie star look. Her smile gave me butterflies. I gave her a quick up-and-down glance, and her body was consistent with the movie star comparison.

I awkwardly blurted out, "So, seriously, would go out with me Friday?"

"Give me your number, and I'll call you. I don't trust you with my number yet, especially after that phony story you told that lady to get her seat near me."

"You knew?"

"Of course, I knew!"

I thought, *This is going to be interesting.* Next dumb question, "Is this considered our first date?"

With no hesitation she shot back, "Hardly. I'll meet you Friday at a jewelry store so we can pick out that ring."

Stunned, I didn't know what to say. I scribbled my home phone number on the back of a Little Italy business card, and as she reached for the card, I took her hand and kissed it gently. I was surprised at how tiny her hands were. Even through her make up I could tell she was blushing. "Call me, soon, please."

The next day when I walked into the house, Mama Maria greeted me with, "Some lady called, Catherine I think she said, and left a number for you to call back."

My mind—and mouth—went into overdrive, "When did she call? Did she say anything else? Did she sound interested?"

"She called around 3 o'clock and asked who I was when I answered. I told her Maria LeoMorte, I think she thought I may have been a wife or girlfriend. How could she sound interested over the phone?"

I wondered if I would look desperate if I called back immediately or should I wait until the evening? To heck with playing it cool, I started dialing with no thought of what I was going to say.

My concerns could wait until tomorrow.She answered. We set up a date. My mind was whirling, but I'm pretty sure I fell asleep smiling. And the rest, as they say, is history.

Chapter VII

The Return of Evil

I arrived at the coffee shop early. What in the world could it be now? What secret did Bunny carry with her now? She had been instrumental in Vince's death—maybe not directly—but was she at least the catalyst of this family disaster.

I intentionally sat where I could see the door, a lesson my father had taught me, and I saw Bunny enter. I was anxious to find out what this was all about.

I waved my hand to signal my location. "Over here Mrs. Dempsey," I called out.

I respectfully scooted a chair out for her.

"A true gentleman just like your father," she remarked.

"My father taught me many valuable lessons."

"He was certainly a good man."

"Yes, he was."

She got right to the point. "In many ways I feel responsible for the death of your brother, Vincent."

"I understand, but what did you want to see me about?"

"I wasn't sure if you understood the backstory behind my son Mickeys' birth, Daniel your student's father?"

"Eventually I was told some of the details about you and Father Parisi."

"My husband, well ex-husband found out in a very strange twist of fate about the fact that he wasn't Mickey's real father." Bunny continued, "Sean took my son to the doctor for his school physical and to get him the necessary shots for school.

Dr. O'Malley was an old family friend, and Sean had done some remodeling work for him. He was a carpenter by trade. As I understand the events of that day, everything was fine, Mickey followed the doctor into the examining room, andfter about twenty minutes the doctor emerged and told Sean everything looked fine, all of Mickey's shot were up to date, and that he'd call in a few days when the blood work came back from the lab.

"That call came at the house later that week. I was working late that day, but Sean was home from work and answered the phone. but I was still downtown working late.

"I didn't find out the detail of that conversation until much later, when Dr. O'Malley confided to me that Sean demanded, 'You aren't to tell anyone about this. No one!' He remembered it this way;

"Sean this is Doctor O'Malley."

"Yes Doctor."

"We've been friends for a long time."

"Yes, we have, is there something wrong?"

"I'm not sure. I have your records here—yours and Bonnie's—and I have here that your blood type is O, and hers is type A."

"So what?"

"Michael's blood type came back as type B. He's not adopted, is he?"

"You know he's not! What are you saying?"

"I'm saying biological parents with type and A and O can't produce a baby with blood type B."

Bunny swallowed hard, then continued, "I had no idea this was all happening, but I did know that Sean harbored ill will towards your family especially against Vincent. He presumed there was something between us after the initial harmless flirting incident when he first met your father and Vincent at the restaurant. Never did I think that Sean's rage would turn into the ghastly murder of poor Vincent."

"It destroyed my parents. My mother was never the same." I continued as Bunny bowed her head in shame, "My mother,

Maria, carried that burden with her until her death. She also seemed to have some other deep secret, a constant shadow of deep darkness at times."

"She was a lovely woman," Bunny remarked.

"So why this meeting? What is it you want?"

"Well, Tony, I don't know where you stand on all this business. I always feared your father might try to hunt Sean down and take revenge on himn. My concern was the continued damage being done to people and their families."

I recited the words taught me by Big Tony. "My father forewarned me many, many times, *Those who hate you won't come after you, they'll go after what you cherish the most.*" In this case he was right."

"For what I knew of your father, he came from a very different culture, a different world."

"He did and was a man of principle, character, and intense beliefs, not always following the letter of the world's law but his traditional law," I said.

"The reason I wanted to talk to you is that, after all these years, I recently received a letter from Sean. He apparently is still in Ireland and from what I can tell in the Dublin area. Ireland doesn't have ZIP codes, they use something called Eircodes that give a postal district number."

"Why should that matter to me?"

"I didn't know if you would ever want to confront him about the death of your brother Vincent, or at least want to know where he was—for your own peace of mind."

"Would it surprise you if I told you I already know where he is?"

"You do? "She shot back.

"Another old saying, *Don't let the same snake bite you twice.* I made it my business to keep track of him."

"Do you have plan?" Bunny asked instantly.

"Ma'am, I always have a plan, but I also know enough to never let anyone know what I'm thinking. I have realistic view of the world, and a big part of that is being prepared for almost any eventuality."

Quietly, I thought how I prided myself on my awareness of my surroundings. My world has always been small, and protecting those closest to me is important. I wondered, *what is this woman's motivation?*

"Mrs. Dempsey, is there anything else you want to talk about? I don't want to be rude, but I have no idea what you expect me to do with this information."

Looking down, she said, "My intentions are honorable, I assure you, Tony. I don't want to cause anymore pain to your family than what has already been inflicted. I have the letter with me if you want it."

"I will take the letter as a matter of mild interest, but I don't really see much coming from it."

The truth was, I thought I could glean a great deal of information from this correspondence which might prove interesting later.

Bunny pressed on, "Would you like me to keep in touch if there are any new developments?"

"If you think the developments are relevant, that would be very much appreciated."

"Again, my most sincere apologies for the trouble I created. It was certainly not intentional. Thanks for meeting me, and if there's anything I can do feel free to contact me. Here's a card with my current information."

"Thanks."

We stood, and she moved toward me and gave me an extra long hug almost the point to of making it uncomfortable. As we released our embrace, she whispered "If you weren't married..."

What? Wow! I watched as she slowly walked away and wondered what else she might know or be thinking.

When I recounted the story to Catherine, I omitted Bunny's parting comment and felt a pang of guilt for having done so. It's not like I was interested, I just didn't want to create questions in my marriage. I had been in a marriage with someone who displayed a penchant for jealousy—it was ugly and destructive.

Memories did come flooding back about Bunny Dempsey's

past history with the LeoMorte family. I mentally questioned how my parents viewed her and if it was disruptive to my mother and father's relationship? Did it create doubt in mom's mind? Did my father regret ever meeting her? I'm sure he did because of the pain of losing his son so senselessly from what was a seemingly harmless friendship. I didn't want to overthink the situation, but I was haunted by occasional thoughts of the effect on my family from my brother Vincent's death at the hands of Sean Dempsey. Was any association with this woman an awakening of *the family curse, Cent' Anni, one hundred years?*

Catherine would periodically get vicious letters—untraceable correspondences filled with ominous threats. I wondered who could be so cruel to this gentle woman? Maybe my ex-wife, Carla Price? It wasn't out of the question.

It hurt my heart to hear the contents of these one-sided threatening letters. I'd always viewed Catherine as on of the kindest, most gentle persons to ever walk the face of the earth, and I know the harsh words and threats worried her, not just for her own safety but for everyone around her.

She asked, "Why would someone send this to me? I've never bothered anyone, I wouldn't intentionally hurt anyone, or even think bad things about people."

"Honey, there's a saying—*hurt people, hurt people.* I think it's true."

The worry on her face was followed with, "Who do you suppose it is? How can we get it to stop?"

Even though I had my suspicions I didn't reveal my theory. "Think back," I encouraged her, "can you think of anyone who would have anything against you?"

"Maybe my ex-husband, but I don't think so?" she said nervously.

"Should we try to get in touch with him to see if there's a clue as to his involvement?"

"No, as mean as he is, I don't think at this point he cares. He's moved on with his life."

Trying to assure her, I offered, "I say just let it go then."

But secretly I was genuinely worried about the whole situation, although since we were together most of the time I certainly felt capable of protecting her and everyone else in my family. I knew how to prioritize my concerns, or at least I thought I did.

My physical condition is that of a normal man of my age. I stay fairly active mentally and physically. My side hustle in the business world kept me mentally nimble, and the frequent fishing and karate were good forms of physical exercise. For a while I was troubled by a lower body ache that developed into a nagging, uncomfortable condition. At Catherine's insistence I made a doctor's appointment with my longtime friend and physician Bob Dressler.

After a routine checkup—at least it seemed routine to me—Bob said, "I don't like the symptoms you're exhibiting. Let's do some blood work and talk in a few days."

I agreed to the blood test and went home thinking it probably wasn't serious. After three days I got a call from Bob.

"Tony, I'm referring you to a specialist, a friend of mine, Dr. Wade Long. Before you start arguing with me, I've already made the appointment. Go see him Friday at 10 AM."

I told Catherine this was just a quick follow up visit, because I knew the true reason would scare her.

When Friday came, I walked into an unfamiliar building, found the office, and was directed to the waiting room. There were the customary forms to fill out, insurance cards to be copied. and then the long wait. I grabbed a seat. Immediately I sensed *the doctor's office smell,* that sterile aroma. For a few nervous minutes I shuffled through a golf magazine, but I couldn't concentrate. At last my name was called.

"The doctor will see you now, Mr. LeoMorte. Did I pronounce that correctly?"

"Yes ma'am"

She ushered me into a cold waiting room with the standard equipment. I could feel my blood pressure rising. Seconds later a very large man entered the room and introduced himself as Dr. Wade Long.

My first thought at shaking hands with this giant of a man was, *I hope I'm not getting the full rubber glove exam.*

"Our friend Dr. Bob says your experiencing some lower abdominal pain."

I played it off as not being severe. "Just a little discomfort from time to time."

"Let's have a look."

After listening to my heart and lungs out came the lube and rubber gloves. *Oh, no!* A few samples were taken, more probing, and I was allowed to return to my normal male dignity.

I endured the examination, glad it was complete, and I was told once again I would be contacted after a few days.

Monday morning the phone rang, and I recognized the voice of Dr. Long's receptionist.

"Mr. LeoMorte, Doctor Long would like to speak with you."

The next voice I heard was that of the doctor. "Mr. LeoMorte, Dr. Long, I'd like you to come back in later today, maybe at the end of my day, let's say five o'clock."

"Why? Is there something I need to know?"

"It'll just take a few minutes. Can you make it?"

Nervously, I responded, "I'll be there."

Now I felt the guilt of not being completely honest with Catherine. How was I going to explain this?

The parking lot was almost empty when I arrived except for a few cars and a black, shiny BMW SUV which I assumed belonged to the doctor.

A quick elevator ride and I was again at the office door. Dr. Long was waiting for me when I walked in.

With a stern look on his face he led me into a small office.

"No sense beating around the bush. I'll get right to the point. My professional diagnosis is you have cancer."

I could feel the blood drain from my face, and my stomach knotted.

"We'll need to do some additional testing at Saint John's hospital to confirm."

I barely heard any more of his words after hearing the dreaded word—*cancer.*

My head was spinning. How was I going to tell Catherine?

With a potentially deadly diagnosis on my mind, I drove slowly toward home. I was going to have to reveal my deception about the second doctor's visit and this awful news of cancer.

Entering the door way I heard Catherine busy in the kitchen.

"How was your doctor's visit?"

"It was okay, I was referred to a new doctor," I called out.

"A new doctor, why?" she questioned.

"My regular doctor had some concerns and sent me to a specialist."

"You didn't tell me that!"

My voice betrayed the shame I felt, "I know, I didn't want you to worry."

"We've always told each other everything," she said as a tear trickled down her cheek.

"I'm sorry, never again, I'll never do that again. I need you to sit down for a minute."

"Sit down? Why, what's wrong?"

"The second doctor thinks I might have cancer."

"Oh my God, no!" Catherine said as she jumped up and moved in to hug me.

"Now just hold on, it's a bit premature to panic. I'm going to be tested again, and then we'll know more. Just calm down," I said knowing no one ever calmed down after hearing those words.

"I'm going with you so I can talk to this doctor," she declared!

Three days later we were sitting at Saint John's Hospital going through a few tests. I was nervous but didn't want Catherine to know it. It seemed like I answered the same questions repeatedly. Poking, prodding, saying "Ah." Examinations, X-rays, paperwork, "Does this hurt?

The ride home was quiet. Neither of us spoke.

The next day the phone rang. It was doctor Long.

"Mr. LeoMorte, Doctor Long here. Good news, it appears that you just have a severe urinary tract infection. A strong dose of antibiotics should clear this up in about a week."

Whew, what a relief. Catherine was right next to me and could hear the doctor's voice.

"Thanks, Doc!"

Catherine and I embraced for what seemed like an hour but was more like a minute. Both of us were overcome with joy and thanks for the answer to our prayers.Another disaster averted. But…

Chapter VIII

The Charmed Life

Like most folks our age we settled into a routine, comfortable but evolving into an inadvertent trap. Daily repeatable schedules consisting of errands, going to the bank, grocery store, grabbing the occasional lunch, walks after supper, and the phone calls from family and friends centered around kids' activities, the weather, and the usual gossip.

I prided myself in knowing everything I could about Catherine, a form of the deepest love, likes, dislikes, favorite flower, colors, clothes sizes, preferences, music and more.

For all practical purposes we were living the dream. Our daily routine was an early wake up, Catherine would rise and turn on the coffee, I enjoyed the luxury of lying there a few extra minutes thinking about the day's activities ahead. It was always my practice to not let my feet hit the floor before saying a brief prayer.

"Good morning, I love you," was my normal greeting.

Catherine's reply, "I love you," was followed by "what do you want for breakfast?"

I always enjoyed the fact that she managed to make every meal special. Breakfast plates garnished with a fresh strawberry, at lunch extra mustard on my sandwich in the form of a heart, at supper carefully prepared hot full meals containing a few of my favorite thing,s and *no* Brussel sprouts or asparagus.

After each meal I was sure to extend the common courtesy of a sincere thank you for my breakfast, lunch, or supper.

"You're welcome," was her common reply, and she made it sound so genuine.

"Do we have anything scheduled for today?"

Catherine would respond, "Is there anything written on the calendar?" We're old school and kept a calendar on the back of the pantry door.

"No commitments. You want to go fishing?"

"I thought maybe we could go see the kids."

I knew there was no "maybe" here and just nodded knowing resistance was futile, the rapid agreement was the preferred acknowledgment. She loved family but especially grandkids.

This was the life I had yearned for, a beautiful woman who was committed to me, pleased me in every way, and who made every emotion make sense. When you find this kind of love it touches your soul. We both loved music, and most of the time when you hear music it's the notes, but in the times of deepest emotion you hear the lyrics. Each sunrise with her was the promise of a new, good day, and each sunset meant peace, reflection, and a hopefully a good sleep.

Every "I love you" could be heard but more important could be felt.

She would randomly say, "I love our time together."

"I do too!"

"What's the adventure for today?" she would ask.

"What would you like to do?" Answer a question with a question, this is a safe formula for the feeling out process of old married folks.

These conversations took place regularly, both of us truly wanted the other to be happy.

"Let's just ride and stop wherever it suits us," I suggested lending itself to a sort of mini adventure.

I'm a different person. I like to believe I did everything with purpose, no wasted motion. She on the other hand was more of a wanderer.

"I want to go places, see things, travel close and far away."

"Don't you ever get tired? "I said with a hint of exhaustion.

"No, I want to live life, I want to make memories with you."

How do you say no to that?

So we would take off, stop at out of the way places, find little shops, restaurants, talk and laugh as if we were school kids ditching classes, carefree… or so it seemed.

As it is with everyone, there's always a hiccup, a bump in the road, life happens. We were content as long as nothing major came along. She was the optimist, I leaned heavily toward being a realist—we in a sense did balanced each other out.

With Easter approaching we decided to attend a sunrise service.

She asked, "I've never been to an outside sunrise service, can we go together?"

"Sure. I've been, it's different, but we'll go."

"What's early for other people is normal for us. It starts at 6 AM."

"We'll be up an hour before that." I chuckled at the thought.

"It'll just take me 45 minutes to get ready, and I'll make you breakfast when we get back."

"Deal," I responded.

The service was going to be beside a lake. We parked, set up camp-style chairs, and waited for the service to begin.

"These look like a lot of nice people," Catherine noted.

My head was always on a swivel, watching everyone and everything around us. Catherine was such a gentle, kind, and trusting soul. Those qualities scared me when we weren't together.

People smiled and casually waved, we introduced ourselves, and one couple actually said, "We know who you are. We're familiar with the LeoMorte clan."

I wasn't sure how to take that.

"We've seen your pictures in the paper," The lady continued.

Uh oh, where were they going with that? I thought.

"We're lifelong residents of the area. Your father was very kind to our family when we ran on hard times, he helped us out insisting that we keep his kindness quiet."

"Yep, that was my father. We refer to it jokingly as secret service." That drew a smile from the couple. "He was a kind person and compassionate to the plight of others," I added.

"We have lost track of the rest of your family," the man commented.

Just about then the service began cutting the conversation off. I kind of welcomed the timing fearing the need to go into details about the other family members.

As the Easter service ended, the couple tossed out the obligatory comment, "We should get together sometime."

Catherine charmingly said, "That would be nice."

I ushered her away quickly to avoid an exchange of information and to get to my much-anticipated breakfast.

Once safely in the confines of the car Catherine questioned me.

"You seemed in a hurry to get away from those people."

"I was. Two things; I like to keep my world small, and I always believed more people usually means more problems. I'm sure they are nice, but we really don't have time for additional social activities, and we barely know them," I cautioned.

"It's okay to expand our social circle," Catherine advised.

"I'm always concerned about people's motivation. Why would they want to get closer to us?"

"I guess we're just different. I like people."

"I just know what people are capable of. By the way, what's for breakfast?" It was an obviously awkward attempt at ending the conversation, and the ride got quiet.

We truly enjoyed our life even in the simplest form; for us the most mundane activities remained fun. We found ourselves laughing at silly things and strange people at the grocery store or wherever we went. Trips into the public were still an adventure, an unplanned lunch date as we maneuvered through traffic, a stop after seeing wild flowers would cause me to jump out and gather a handful to put in vase back at the house, all these things kept us smiling. While I had traveled extensively, Catherine was limited in her early life by work, children, and dedication to responsibilities. She constantly hungered for travel, new places, sights and sounds of distant lands. I was content to stay local and spend lazy days on the water.

Invariably the topic would arise, "What would you think about flying to Italy?" she asked out of the blue.

I responded, "As opposed to driving?"

A snap of the head in my direction and being stared at over the rims of her glasses sent a clear signal that my comment was ill-advised and my humor unappreciated.

"We could see ancestral family places, experience how other people live, new food, culture, and architecture."

"Maybe," I said almost under my breath.

"Why not now or at least soon?" she pressed on.

"I still have a few job responsibilities."

"What's the point of having the money and the time if we're not using either?"

This was chance to utter the famous phrase, "We'll see." *Oops*, that was the opening she was looking for, soon there were travel brochures and maps scattered across an end table.

She, being the dreamer, me being the highly organized partner, brought us to the when, where, and how conversation.

"Where should we go first?" she asked with the spirit of adventure in her voice.

"I know, let's make a list." I replied in a moderately sarcastic tone.

"You mean like a bucket list?"

"Not really, more of an organizational type thing."

A frown came over her face signaling I was taking all the fun out of the task. I quickly pivoted. "This way we can dream about all the faraway places to travel."

That turned her frown upside-down. Good save by me! I always wanted her to be happy.

"I love the look of Ireland—historic, green landscape and so many traditions." She had Irish in her background, but it was a bitter thought for me because of the atrocity of Vince's untimely demise and the culprit fleeing to his homeland, Ireland.

"Would that be you first choice?" I asked hoping to dissuade her.

"Gosh, I don't know."

Frustrated I said, "You always seem too indecisive. You freeze when you need to make a decision." I knew it was a mistake as soon as I heard the words leave my mouth.

Catherine sat in silence, wounded.

I blurted out, "We're all different. You just need more time to process information, do research, and come to a conclusion."

"Nice try! But that wasn't very nice."

That's as harsh as a return volley as I would ever get from my Catherine.

Again, I suggested, "Let's make a wish list of all the places we'd like to visit, then narrow it down and prioritize it as to in what order we'd like to go."

"Are you making fun of me?" Catherine asked in an angry tone.

"No, just suggesting an organized approach. We can get a large folder, collect information, and plan it all out."

Our day was winding down. I always looked forward to bedtime. As we slid beneath the sheets, Catherine was ready for sleep, and I took this time for a late night session I referred to as *pillow talk*. At times she would engage; at other times it was announced, "I'm ready to go to sleep."

I found it amusing to occasionally leave what I termed a *pillow present*. I would sneak into our bedroom and leave some nonsensical item on Catherine's pillow. A can of soup, a piece of candy, a chocolate chip cookie, and then sometimes I would cut a heart out of a paper towel and scrawl a message on it. The food items went unappreciated; the notes always drew an admiring look and sometimes lead to spontaneous romance.

I was like a little kid; I couldn't help but giggle waiting in anticipation of her arrival when I placed the pillow present carefully on her side of the bed. Hiding in the shadows and trying to muffle my laugh, I couldn't contain my excitement. Often, I had to remind myself, *If you're the only person laughing it's probably not that funny.*

Most times we were on the same sleep schedule, the late-night conversation went like this.

She initiated, "Are you tired?"

"Just a few more minutes, I want to see how this show ends."

"No, I'm tired. You've seen this a hundred times. You can repeat the dialogue from memory."

"Okay, just one minute," I pleaded

After we entered the room and slipped into our sleep attire, I felt the need to add one more thing.

"Can I tell you a secret?"

"Okay, but make it quick."

"I've fallen in love hundreds of times."

"You have?" she sat straight up in bed and asked, surprised at the admission.

"Yep, every morning when I wake up next to you."

"Awe! That's so sweet. Now go to sleep."

There's an undeniable peace at the end of the day, the house falls silent, there's the warmth exchanged from our bodies touching, and then the promise of a new day. This is what life should be like.

Chapter IX

Love and Loss

If loving someone or something could save them, nothing would ever die. Almost embarrassed by my sensitivity, I took losing people and even pets extremely hard. Unlike the persona my family projected, I was affected deeply by what might be seen as seemingly insignificant things as well as what to most people, life altering circumstances.

Even as a child I took losses hard—it seemed like it was harder for me than anyone else.

Where pets were concerned while others referred to them as dogs, deep down I believed they were family. German Shepherds were the preferred and only breed in our home. The names revealed my father's sense of humor, even if it was subtle or well disguised. For example, there was J. Edgar and Al. J. Edgar was named after the F.B.I. director J. Edgar Hoover, and Al was named after Italian gangster Al Capone. My father favored Al and made sarcastic comments to J. Edgar while still being civil to him. I'd see him smile as he teased each of our furry friends. The pups were always happy to see us and ran around the yard as we entered the fence.

I only viewed them as full of life and very protective, never as mortal creatures and never thinking that one day they would be gone. First J. Edgar died, probably of natural causes associated with old age, which left Al lonely, and eventually one evening he just went to sleep and didn't wake up. I really think he died of a broken heart. Others that followed, Rocky, Rico, and Samurai—the joy they brought outweighed their eventual departure, but for me at least, it was still very difficult. The concept of death lingered, and I vacillated between an almost morbid fascination and fear. I struggled to understand the finality, the cruel disappearing act, one moment you're here and then in an instant, you're not.

There were other significant personal struggles that punctuated my life.

I took the end of my first marriage hard, I foolishly thought marriage was for life. The circumstances surrounding my divorce were difficult to get past. I learned in life, especially when enduring painful things, sometimes you just get past them, but you never get over them.

After a few years into our marriage it seemed Carla was unhappy all the time. She suggested counseling to which I agreed hoping to bring our marriage back to life. During our early counseling, I started watching everything more closely. I looked for clues as to how to make my wife happy again. I complimented her on her new wardrobe, I noted her weight loss and the change of her hair color as well as the style. She'd even gotten new sexier underwear. This renewal seemed to energize us both. I believed this was an honest effort on her part to renew our bond.

Things seemed to be progressing slowly, but there was less arguing. I thought it was genuine progress, but then wondered if it was just disguised ambivalence because she didn't care anymore. I got my answer one Saturday afternoon when I was inside helping to prepare a work file while Carla was outside in a lounge chair with her cordless phone and a wine cooler. She was smiling then laughing on a call that seemed to go on and on.

She hung up and came inside. "I'm going out for a while."

There was no indication as to where she was going or for how long, which seemed a little unusual.

"Where are you going?" I asked.

"Out, I'm going out! You know the opposite of in! Is that okay?" She shot back.

"Who were you talking to?"

"Just a girlfriend of mine," she replied sheepishly.

"I'm going to take a shower and then I'll be gone for a while. I don't know what time I'll be back."

This new phone had a feature marked as *redial*. Not familiar with the feature, for some unknown reason I curiously hit the button, and the phone made a series of beeps followed by a male voice answering, "Hello."

Surprised, but astute enough, I quickly made up a name and said, "Hello, is this Mike Cummings?"

"No, this is Ronnie Newsome," was the reply.

I asked, "Is this 895-2790?"

"No, it's 895-3890."

"Must have the wrong number. Sorry to have bothered you." With a shaky hand I quickly scribbled down the unfamiliar name and number. My world stopped but also seemed to be spinning out of control at the same time.

Wow, I thought. *Now that was very suspicious.* I went into denial trying to convince myself this wasn't really happening.

About twenty minutes later Carla came out dressed up in a black, revealing outfit sure to attract attention.

"Wow, you sure you look nice." I commented

"Yeah, whatever, see ya later." Out the door she went.

My mind was racing. I looked through our room for clues but turned up nothing. Stomach churning, I checked the phone book on a hunch, and there they were the names Ronnie and Crystal Newsome. They lived in the area, but that's all I knew.

Usually I was keenly aware of every detail of things going on around me. Now I routinely checked the odometer of Carla's Corvette and watched for any clue as to what was happening. I spied on her phone calls, watched the mail, and made note of times she left, came back, and what she wore.

Then with an unconvincing tone, out of the blue Carla asked me, "Are you cheating on me?"

"Am I cheating on you? I was wondering that about you," I said, astounded at the bold question.

"If you are, I could get half of everything you have or get a good lawyer and get more than half!"

That moment turned the tide. My singular thought was, *You should have never said that. Gloves off now, this is a battle for survival.*

"Sorry to disappoint you, but I'm faithful to you." I replied menacingly.

"Okay, just checking."

Now the personal war had started.

I had an optometrist appointment the next day. As I was sitting in the waiting room, my eye doctor came out escorting his previous patient. He saw me and walked over to me saying he wanted to introduce me to this man.

"This is Tony LeoMorte. Tony this is Charles Patterson. He's a private detective."

This guy had the look of a serious man—tall, square-shouldered, the appearance of someone not to be trifled with under and circumstances.

"Interesting, do you have a business card?" I asked the man.

"I do," was the reply

"Nice to meet you. Thanks for the card."

I tucked the card into my wallet and went about my business. This was perfect. I knew the snoopy Carla and her habits, I left my wallet out and pulled the card part way out so she would see it. Sure enough she fell for it, the wallet had been moved, the card likely read and replaced, now to wait.

Before anything came up about the business card, I received a phone call from a high school friend of mine.

"Hey man, just a heads up if you're catting around you should be a little more discreet."

"What do you mean?"

"I saw that convertible Corvette you drive outside Coral Courts, that motel on highway 44."

"Are you sure it's the same car?" I asked.

"Yeah, that custom pinstripe is a dead giveaway, and I've seen it there the last two Thursdays."

"Okay, thanks." My stomach ached at this news. My suspicions were now confirmed, I felt that knot in my stomach that comes with level of bad news.

I don't like confrontation, but admittedly I'm good at it. When I arrived home, it was Carla and me, time for the showdown.

"Just so you know, I'm aware of what's going on," I said with confidence.

The blood drained from her face. "What is it you think is going on?" she meekly replied.

"I know where you've been going, what you've been doing, and with who. You accused me of cheating while you were doing it!"

"I haven't been doing anything."

I could hear the panic in her voice and see the guilt written all over her face.

There was a roaring in my ears, and I struggled, vacillating between the emotions of anger, hate and fear…fear of the unknown. Anger was winning.

"Oh, I think you have." I said as I sailed the detective's business card across the table, for the dramatic effect and proof of my suspicions. "I've been having you followed."

"No, you haven't," she replied almost in the form of a question.

"I have, and I even have pictures. You should have been a little more careful."

She took the bait. Now to ramp it up a bit. "Does his wife know about you yet?"

A blank stare and no response to my question, she wore the look of the hopelessly trapped quarry.

"You know I haven't been happy for a long time. We live in this stupid house, with half your family and have no privacy.

They hear our arguments, our conversation, even us having sex. I have to wonder if everyone is listening."

"That's making love, not having sex!"

"No, it's just having sex. I don't love you anymore."

That hurt, but I knew it was true. The door slammed as she left, and I could hear the tires squealing as she sped out of the driveway.

I picked up the phone and called a mutual friend Dorothy to find out what she might know.

"Dorothy? Tony. I just had it out with Carla. I know everything." I waited, and she slowly replied.

"I'm so sorry. I wanted to tell you. I felt so guilty." *Another co-conspirator,* I thought. The charade worked again as she spilled out more sordid details.

"Why did *you* feel guilty?"

"I let her and David use my house. When she said, *he'll never catch me; he trusts me too much,* I knew I couldn't be a part of it anymore. I told them they couldn't use my house as a hideaway any longer."

Dorothy was spewing it all out now." She was coming over to meet up with him once a week."

"What else do you know about him." I asked.

"He's married and has two kids. And there's another guy too." she continued.

"There is?" I asked stunned by this news.

"Yes, a guy whose last name is Newsome."

"Ronnie Newsome? He works at the Sunset country club doesn't he."

I dropped to my knees; I felt nauseous, it wasn't one guy, it was at least two. If there were more, I didn't want to know it. How did I not see this? My complete trust was used against me! I was conflicted between the feelings of being betrayed and being stupid.

Now I came to the full realization I had been living with someone I didn't even know. I began to plot my revenge; I'd catch them in the act. *Then what?*

Carla arrived back home, and I sought the privacy of the outside. She followed me out and immediately took on a haughty, arrogant attitude.

"Ronnie and I are going to get married and start a family."

I'm sure this was meant to hurt me, but at this point I was way past hurt—I was angry.

"Don't you think you ought to end one marriage before you start another one?" I sarcastically shot back.

"I'm just asking you to keep it quiet. I'll leave quietly and just take the car and some cash if you don't tell anyone."

"You'll leave with some cash, but no car. That's cost of cheating."

"Okay, I don't care, I just want out." She was on a mission.

"So, Newsome's wife doesn't know. How about the other guy's wife? Does she know?" I asked. "Does Newsome know about the other guy?"

She knew I was on to her now. "What?" she responded with a panicked look on her face. The change of facial expression and body language showed the shock of now knowing I knew much more than she imagined.

"Yeah, I know about at least two. So, here's how this is going down. You sleep in the spare bedroom tonight and be gone tomorrow. I'll write you check for $4,000—a thousand dollars for each year we were married."

"I'm not doing that."

"You're choice. I'll start calling wives tomorrow," I warned.

"Okay, okay. Just don't say anything. I just want out."

In matter of a few months, Carla's world fell apart. After being dumped by both of her lovers, she made a desperate phone call to me. "I can't do this anymore," she pleaded. "I want to come home."

"Sorry," I replied. "As my father says, "Don't let the same snake bite you twice."

Click.

She went back to seeking her next husband. A *gentleman*

ten years younger than her duped her into a short courtship and then marriage. Not long after he showed his true colors, cheating, drinking, and drugging. Her Prince Charming turned into a rebound nightmare. I confess I took guilty pleasure in the whole thing. As far as his infidelity, I relished the thought that she got a dose of her own medicine.

In a subsequent phone call, I couldn't resist. "You got what you wanted; do you want what you got?"

There were people whose loss haunted me. I continually recognized that the concept of death was difficult for me to deal with at any time under any circumstances. I still questioned, *How is it you're here and then gone, just a lifeless form, a shell of a human?* Death had become a common acquaintance that I never was able to fully accept. I saw other examples as troubling. Buried in the headlines of the *St. Louis Globe-Democrat* newspaper was a headline; "St. Louis Zoo reports that Leo the lion has died." This served as a grim reminder that our legal name, LeoMorte, translated into dead lion. Sometimes I just wanted my mind to take a vacation from the pall of death that seemed to hang around our family.

The threat of the possible return of the curse loomed large and was continually just below the surface. Crazy as it sounds even when things were going well, there existed that mindset of, *Yeah but what about tomorrow*, or the constant fear that something would upset the apple cart.

One bright light for us was the constant addition of grandchildren. For a few years it was just two who I had christened with nicknames, Thomas, "Thomas the Train," and Caroline, aka "Cookie," who were frequent visitors. I'm not sure who had more fun the children, me, or Catherine. We'd play board games, throw the whiffle ball, sing songs, color, and gorge ourselves on unhealthy snacks, all these being the joys of grandparenthood.

Just when the little ones passed the diaper stage it seemed

like there was another one on the way. The number settled at four when Oliver and Amber decided to close up shop. No more children. We continually guided, advised, and watched over our extended family, keeping the theme alive that *family is everything*. We had worldly lessons and the wisdom that comes with experience to offer those around us.

With family comes worry, but in my life maybe it's just a byproduct of genuine love.

Chapter X

Lessons I Lived By

Memories of my younger life stood the test of time and served me well. After hearing multiple times, "Children should be seen and not heard," I got the message, but I listened, watched, and remembered. It must have been an Italian thing to be impatient and swift to respond, because it seemed to be the pervasive sentiment. A verbal warning, the *look*, or a swat in whatever area was closest were the most likely outcomes for any indiscretion.

Respect for family or those who appeared powerful, coupled with a healthy dose of fear kept me vigilant and had me cowering in anticipation of the repercussions for the actions of my siblings or those around me. Eyes were normally trained on my father for a reaction, that was generally the rule. To me it always looked like when someone reacted immediately in times of tension that would come back to bite them.

In one such instance I watched as two of my father's associates had words that turned into a heated argument ending with one of the combatants pulling a knife and stabbing the other. I watched in horror as the injured man was rushed from the building and ushered into the backseat of a big black Cadillac. Tires squealing, they were gone in seconds.

My father viewed this as a *teachable moment* and calmly said, "Now you see, that was very unnecessary."

I was still bugeyed at what had just happened. "That was crazy, like out of a gangster movie!"

"Don't say gangster."

"Why couldn't they just talk about whatever it was, or just walk away?" I wondered out loud.

My father replied, "They let emotions and stupidity take over. They handled it all wrong, you should have noticed, too, that the veins in the attacker's neck were bulging—a sign of anger. Another clue was the watch on his left arm indicating most likely he was right-handed. The other man let him get too close."

In amazement I asked, "You saw all that? Wow! What should they have done?"

"Here's a valuable lesson, Son. I call it the 24-hour rule, wait 24 hours before you reply or react. If you feel the same after 24 hours do what you think you should."

"Now what will happen?" I wondered.

"They'll either negotiate a peace, go before a mediator, or one will kill the other in the name of honor. There's no honor in that!"

"Dad, what's a mediator?"

"Someone who will advise opposing parties as to what to do to come to a civilized, non-violent resolution. Do you understand?"

"I guess so." I was still confused.

My father continued, "Resorting to violence is unnecessary most of the time. You have to think and use some sense when you're an adult, a leader, or have people looking to you for guidance. You should also be willing to compromise, in a sense let other people think that they win. Don't back anyone into a corner, leave them wiggle room. Once you backed someone into a corner there's only one way out. Do you understand?"

I didn't know what to say. I still was stunned by the ease with which people attacked each other, and there was a lot for me to process.

"Remember, listen carefully to people when they're mad, they'll say what they've been thinking for a long time. Think about what they said and how they said it."

On another occasion my father explained to me that power and money should be used to benefit others. "I have no interest in people fearing me. I would rather be respected than feared. People who fear you will try to take you down or hurt you. People who respect you will be loyal to you even in your absence."

That made sense to me, and at some point I realized that my father was wise in business but more importantly in the ways of the world.

Another point he made was how to appropriately apologize.

"If you're wrong, say, "I'm sorry," but—first make sure you're wrong. Offer to make it right, apologize sincerely, if it requires repayment of money or a pledge to not repeat the behavior then do so. It's not a sign of weakness to apologize. Think hard before you promise—be a person of your word."

"What if the person doesn't accept your apology?" I asked.

"Then be satisfied you've done all you can do to make it up to them and move on, but don't trust that person anymore. Avoid them, watch out for them, they'll wait to take revenge on you. The world is a cruel place not meant for those of weak mind or body."

"How did you learn all this?"

"I watched and listened. I also realized very little is as it appears to be on the surface. If people lie or steal or mistreat others, know that they'll also do it to you. I found in my own case, if there's any doubt about a decision…don't do it."

During these serious conversations I did what I now refer to as *using my mental highlighter* to memorialize these bits of wisdom.

I had an interesting childhood to say the least.

Many years later as I navigated through life, I was visited by a member of a longtime family nemesis, a never-before-seen FBI agent came to my door.

"Mr. LeoMorte, Tony LeoMorte?"

"That's me, what can I do for you?"

"My name is Robert Coleman; I was interested in talking to you about a rather delicate matter."

"Of course, you are," I replied flippantly.

This guy was textbook FBI field agent; to the trained eye you could see it from a mile away. Drab olive-green suit, cheap brown shoes, and a knock-off watch. He was tanned with the exception of the white outline of his hair indication a fresh haircut, white button-down Oxford shirt with obligatory red tie indicating, "I'm in control." Oh yeah, this guy was a law dog.

"May I come in?"

"If you insist, but I thought all this nonsense stopped after my father died," I said exhausted with the process.

"This is in reference to a Dominic LeoMorte, your brother, I believe," he explained.

"Whatever he's done it has nothing to do with me!" I snapped back. "Let's move into my office." I walked a step behind him.

The agent moved towards an old brown leather wingback chair that clearly showed its age.

"Not that chair. That was my father's chair. We don't use it out of respect for him."

"I can assure you I'm not going to hurt it." He insisted.

"I know you're not because you're not going to use it." I barked back. First sign you're in control is having a person follow your directives. He silently settled into a rickety old wooden chair and began speaking.

"I believe I may hold some information that may interest you, a few facts you should be aware of at this time."

"Okay, what have you got?"

"I'm assuming this was prior to your birth, but there was a very serious incident involving one of our agents and your mother."

"Sir, my mother was not involved in any family business!" was my angry response.

"This was discovered after an intense investigation; I can assureyou, you *will* want to know," he continued.

"Go on."

"Obviously, you're aware of your brother Dominic's incarceration."

"Which one, there's been several."

"It became state policy to collect DNA samples from convicted felons, of which your brother qualified, as I'm sure you well know. During the eventual DNA profile, it came to out attention that your brother's DNA didn't match the ancestry DNA sample of your father."

"How would you have access to my father's DNA?"

"We retrieved it with a search warrant, then by following him and getting multiple samples from items he used at his businesses, restaurants, and other places he frequented."

"So what's your point?"

"One of our agents turned out to be a bad cop. You might say he went rogue."

"I don't see the connection."

"Under heavy pressure with the threat of a full Internal Affairs investigation, this former FBI agent, Michael "Mike" Collins, confessed to a most heinous crime. He came to your family home alone; this is never the policy of the FBI. We travel in pairs to avoid any impropriety, to witness everything and for our own protection."

"Where is this going?" I asked impatiently.

"By his own admission Collins came to your family home, alone with the intention of harming your father. He hated him and wasn't satisfied to let the FBI do its work. He hatched a plot to take matters into his own hands. When he found your mother alone, he forced her into a bedroom and raped her. He made snap a decision and felt justified to vent his frustration in a horrific way. He figured your mother, whether from shame or fear of what your family would do if they found out, would keep silent. Obviously, she was willing to suffer the humiliation and pain so your father or his henchmen wouldn't seek retribution."

"Are you sure about all this?"

"Yes Sir. Collins, when confronted with a lie detector test, made a full admission. Your mother must have been a strong and brave woman," the agent said.

My only reply was, "She was." But my mind was racing. I

thought, *So, she lived engulfed by the darkness of this secret the rest of her life.*

This just confirmed what I had always suspected about Dominic, that he was so different that the rest of us, and now I knew the reason.

"Sorry to deliver such troubling news," he said, feigning concern.

"What ever became of this Mike Collins?" I slyly asked.

"That's another mystery. We believe he didn't want to face the consequences of his actions, and he found a way to disappear. That's not an easy thing to accomplish when dealing with the FBI."

Deep down I wondered how long this would have gotten past my father, but I also knew he was too sharp for that. I was disappointed too at how my mother could by omission, not reveal something as vial as this to Dad.

"I guess your father really didn't get over on the FBI, at least in this instance he never knew."

"What a screwed up thing to say! Nobody, and I mean nobody got anything over on my father! My father was a tactician of the highest order. He anticipated everyone's move and was six moves ahead of everybody."

"Well, Mr. LeoMorte, in this case it certainly didn't seem he was aware of anything," he replied with a smirk.

"I think it's best you leave now, Mr. Coleman," I said as I escorted him to the door.

"Sorry to bring you such devastating news, sir. Have a good rest of your day," he said sarcastically.

As Coleman and his partner, who had waiting in the car, pulled away, I thought, *You fool. You didn't know Tony LeoMorte, or my mother.*

The all mighty FBI would never be able to figure out what happened to the despicable former FBI agent Mike Collins. I pieced the events together, and eventually I discovered the truth.

My parents were honest with each other all the time. My mother couldn't live with the guilt about how Dominic was conceived. At some point she told my father, but to this day I could tell you Dad never showed the least bit of animosity towards Dom, mostly I'm sure because regardless of the ugly truth of how it happened, he was still part of my mother. He wouldn't do anything to hurt her. My father was strict with all of us, including Dominic, but also accepted him in spite of all of his antics. I think the loss of my murdered oldest brother, Vince, also was a reminder of how precious life was.

Family life was indeed precious, but all bets were off if you harmed anyone close to Big Tony LeoMorte. This in my mind was most evident in my father's patient handling of the FBI agent Mike Collins. Like an apex predator, he waited until the time was right—he waited and watched.

Tony LeoMorte could walk in and own the room or blend in like a chameleon. He gathered and stored information like a human computer.

The day my mother came to him tearfully and bared her soul as to what happened, my father listened, and his mind began to calculate a plan of action.

First came a rock-solid identification of the culprit, then formulate a very specific game plan, options, possibilities, barriers, and the eventual desired outcome. Patience.

Nobody could predict my father's actions, not that he didn't have any routines, it was just his mantra, "I let people act, and then I react." Life was a chess game to him; he was truly a tactician. Rare were the times when you could elicit an automatic response from him. One of his core beliefs was to "Give it 24 hours; if you still feel the same way you can respond in an appropriate way." His modus operandi was to gather information and formulate a well thought out game plan, prepare for every eventuality.

Fearfully, my mother approached my father about Dominic's traumatic conception. She was embarrassed for having been duped and ashamed for not being able to fight off the perpetrator.

"I should have known when he showed up alone—they never did that," she said tearfully.

"You're too kind, Maria. You've lived your life trusting people. I'm the opposite. People have to earn my trust and I never drop my guard, I can't afford to, too many people depend on me."

"I know that about you, my Tony, but that has to be a hard way to live."

"This is a hard world. It doesn't tolerate the weak, stupid, or unprepared."

"I was afraid to tell you for a couple of reasons. First I didn't want you to take vengeance on this monster that did this to me, and second I didn't want you to treat Dominic differently than the other children."

"You know this will create a gigantic inner conflict for me, but no matter what, Dominic was a part of you. Because of that he's also a part of this family."

"So, you can let it go and live with it as we have so far?" my mother asked.

"I can do whatever I have to in order to keep our lives happy and consistent with the values of our ancestors. Eventually everybody gets what they deserve, whether it's on earth or in the next life," my father responded, masking his true intentions.

This was merely a clever, if less than honest dodge on my father, Big Tony's, part.

He waited. Eventually he would execute a genius and meticulous plan of retribution. Nobody but nobody could get away with something like this. Our family honor was at stake. Hell's fury would descend on the violator.

What really happened? He waited, and when the time was right Collins was snatched, killed, taken to the cemetery where there was a freshly dug grave, and buried unceremoniously in the same spot. No one would ever know.

It seemed unnecessary to me to tell Dominic that in truth he was a half-brother.

Chapter XI

Where There's a Will

One of the most consistent values Big Tony LeoMorte believed and lived was, "Never reward bad behavior." This was a guiding principle that was unwavering in his mind and also in his actions.

It was never more evident than in the plan he devised to take revenge on the rogue FBI agent who had defiled his wife in the worst way possible; rape.

Once aware of the transgression against his wife, Tony began a meticulously detailed plan of action to address this devastating event.

The culprit identified, Tony used his connections to find out every detail concerning his adversary. Mike Collins was in Big Tony's crosshairs and part of the plot was that the intended target never knew they were being set up. Twent-four hour surveillance was conducted, every move tracked—like most people, this creep was a creature of habit. From home, to work, to the gym, out to eat, trips to the grocery store—everything you would expect from a person in a high-profile position in law enforcement, a regimented lifestyle. He had one flaw in his routine that would prove to be fatal.

In this case the seclusion and darkness would be the friend of the vigilantes. It was after a late night trip to a secluded park for a romantic rendezvous—this cad was having an affair with a married woman, and they would regularly met in the darkest recesses of this park to carry on their physical activities.

The revenge-minded trio assembled by Tony waited for the lovers to part ways, then sprang into action. A quick attack on the unsuspecting agent had him stuffed into the backseat of a stolen car before he knew what was happening—a stolen car that couldn't be connected to the group, gloved hands to prevent the occupants from being identified.

"Do you have any idea of who I am?" the philandering agent asked in a self-righteous tone.

"We know exactly who you are."

"Whatever you have in mind, there is no way you can get away with this," blurted out the cad.

"I'm only going to tell you once—shut up," demanded one of the henchmen.

The car sped off to begin the one-way ride for Collins. A pillow case over his head meant he couldn't identify anyone if he were to escape, but it also served to ramp up the fear he surely felt regarding his unknown fate. After a 30 minute ride to a more remote location, Collins was gruffly removed from the backseat.

The next voice Collins heard sounded vaguely familiar.

"So, you thought you got away with it, huh?" Big Tony bellowed.

With his head still covered Colins innocently asked, "Tony LeoMorte, is that you? Got away with what?"

"Your visited to my house years ago," Tony replied as the pillowcase was snatched off.

"I don't know what you mean?"

This insolence earned the rapist a backhanded. "Maybe that will refresh your memory."

Nose bleeding, Collins replied, "I don't know what you're talking about."

"I'm talking about you raping my wife, you spineless coward. Did you think you were going to get away with it, that you wouldn't have to pay for it?" The explosive angry now evident in the volume of Tony's voice. "There are so many ways you could be made to pay for your attack on my wife, not to mention your relentless harassment of my family. You're going to suffer!"

"I swear to God I didn't—"

His response was cut short by a swift kick to the groin, a not so subtle sign of Big Tony's disdain for this rat and his actions.

"You're never going to hurt anyone else again."

"You'll never get away with hurting me," remarked Collins.

Tony's eyes glaring, he responded, "Hurt you? I'm not going to hurt you. I'm going to kill you! But first, I'm going to relieve you of your weapon of choice, your *junk*, as a small part of your death sentence."

"Killing me won't change the past. What can I do to make it right?" begged the coward.

"There's nothing you can do. It's what I'm going to do to make it right."

"Just let me go. I'll leave, and you'll never see or hear from me ever again."

"No, I'm leaving now, and you're not. And I can guarantee that while I may occasionally think of you, I will never, ever see or hear from you. Neither will anybody else."

Tony looked at his accomplices and gave a nod which signaled them to proceed the plan.

"No wait, Mr. LeoMorte please wait, what are you going to do?"

"Me, I'm going home to my nice warm bed where I will lay next to my wife."

"What about me?"

"You? You've got a date with the devil. *Arrivederci.*"

As he strolled away, Tony could hear the agonizing screams from the physical pain the culprit was feeling. Tony thought, *This was the man who created the same kind mental haunting pain in my wife's mind, now this miscreant knows what it feels like to be helpless, doomed to suffer, to pay the ultimate price for his crime.*

Another part of the intricate plan was to fully conceal the retribution, making it less likely to ever be discovered. Tony read the obituaries in the newspaper and chose a cemetery with easy access, no cameras, and the location of a most recent burial.

His instructions were, once the deed was done, to wait until late night, and under the veil of darkness, take the body of his nemesis to the recently dug grave of an everyday citizen, who in death would act as a sort of a silent accomplice to the revenge plot, then they would remove several feet of the fresh dirt, throw the body in, cover it with lime to make it disappear faster, and cover it back up. No one would ever notice the addition of another body to a fresh grave site.

I had mixed emotions years later when my father revealed the sinister retribution taken on the man that changed our lives forever. I never saw my father as the same man.

A reworded phrasing of a common quote, "Where there's a will, there's a way," was the twisted Italian version of it, "Where there's a will, there's a relative." Greed does strange things to people, especially some family members.

As per Big Tony's wishes it had become time for the final execution of his will and distribution of funds. He left very specific instructions, and I knew my father was a man who always acted with purpose and great attention to detail. Often, he was pensive, very deep in thought, and I many times wondered if he was processing information at that moment with the goal of eventually formulating another plan or a response.

On one occasion I became acutely aware of my father studying his business ledgers intensely. He would look, turn a page, reference another set of business records and go back to the first book. He did this repeatedly, and it produced a troubled look on his face. After about an hour, he closed the books and let out an audible sigh. He noticed me sitting there, we exchanged serious glances, I had questions but waited for him to speak. As much as I wanted to, I didn't ask anything, and he didn't offer any explanation as he rose from the desk and slammed the books into a home wall safe.

With most people when they get loud, you should be frightened. Not so with Big Tony LeoMorte. When he gets quiet, it's time to worry.

I laugh inside when I hear someone utter the tired old adage, "It's not the money, it's the principle." My belief, the majority of the time, it's *not* the principle…it's the money!

In my father's world, there was a code of behavior. You didn't mess with another man's wife or his family, you didn't steal, snitch, lie, or conspire against the head of the mob or the head of the household.

Leaders have many things in common. One aspect of leadership is knowing what and when to ask certain questions. In Tony LeoMorte's case, he would only ask questions when he already knew the answers. I had seen this many times. He'd look in your eyes to see if there was deception, or watch to see if you turned your gaze away, or hesitated to answer, stumbled on your words, or changed your story.

"I'm only going to ask you once, and I'd better get the truth," he would thunder.

In pouring over the books, he had noticed some irregularities in the reporting. This man of limited formal education could compute five-digit numbers in his head all day long. Along with his mathematical acumen, he had what would be a natural, undocumented degree in street smart psychology, all the while being very mentally nimble.

He arranged a private, unassuming casual meeting with my sister, Mary Rose. To put her at ease he visited her at her home where she would be most comfortable. In a carefully orchestrated conversation, he began the interrogation.

"Mary Rose, my daughter, bookkeeper and first born girl, how are you?"

"It's good to see you, Papa. Can I get you a glass of wine, cup of coffee, anything?"

"No, thank you. How are my grandchildren, the *bambini*?

"Oh, they're great."

If Mary Rose had been on her game, she'd have recognized my father was making her comfortable and disarming her. I knew my father in ways she did not!

"How's everything here, your home, your husband? You got everything you need?" He said, setting her up.

"Oh sure. We're good, all is good."

"It just seems like you've got a lot of nice cars, jewelry, going on expensive vacations—I hope you're not getting in over your head financially."

"No, Papa. We've got plenty of money."

"It's important to save too. You have to be careful with your money. The trouble with money is there's always somebody who wants to take it away from you," he slyly remarked.

"I wouldn't let anyone take money away from me. You take from me, you're taking from my family, my kids! No way!"

"Yeah, that would be unforgivable. By the way, how's Dominic, how do you think he's doing financially?" he probed further.

"Dom? Papa, he only has what you pay him. I don't think he's involved in any shady activities like he was before, but even now I still don't trust him; I wouldn't believe anything he says."

He watched as it seemed Mary Rose showed signs of discomfort, squirming in her seat.

"Well, I have to be going. I just wanted to stop in for a few minutes and check on you," said Tony, bidding farewell.

With his banking connections, my father could get any information on anybody in the city. Monday morning inquires brought him some sad news. Tracking Mary Rose's accounts, they showed a long standing and consistent weekly deposit in ascending amounts over a fairly long period of time. Tony thought this was significant because unscrupulous persons, especially those pulling monetary fraud, begin with small numbers first to see if there's any discovery by the victims. If all remains quiet, then they ramp up the amounts secreted away. Checking profits against deposited by bookkeeper / accountant, Mary Rose showed a correlation between money missing from the business along with identical amounts deposited in her secret savings account. She was embezzling money! Further investigation showed direct transfers from her account into an account identified only as DL Enterprises. It didn't take a genius to figure out DL was Dominic LeoMorte. They were in it together! Most likely Dominic somehow discovered the scheme Mary Rose was pulling and demanded hush money.

Betrayed by family? Unforgivable!

Money makes people do strange things, but the reality is that it's just paper with numbers on it. Money is only as good as how you can use it, and it can only be used once. Money should be used wisely.

My father came to me, and in accordance with his wishes, we rented two huge safe deposit boxes, at different bank locations, both under his name with my name on the bank card as the only other authorized person who could access the contents. My instructions were that these boxes were to be used to hold the cash inheritance for both Mary Rose and Dominic. His will stated that on the two year anniversary of his death, the contents of the boxes were to be distributed to my siblings. Sister Angelina, sworn to a vow of poverty, was aware that a huge sum of money, several hundred thousand dollars was to be bequeathed to the church or school at which she was located at the same time.

As executor, it was my father's wish that I receive my inheritance, an astronomical amount of cash immediately upon his demise. We all knew large sums of cash were awaiting us with the instructions to spend it slowly and wisely to avoid the intense scrutiny and money trail that followed our family.

The date approached for the opening of the safe deposit boxes. Both Mary Rose and Dominic had been advised to not tell anyone of their impending windfall and to bring a very large travel bag to transport their inheritance. I was to meet them separately, an hour apart with Mary Rose going first.

On time and as scheduled, Mary Rose met me at the National Bank of St. Louis. I met her at her car door.

"Good morning, are you ready?"

"I am so ready; I miss Papa, but it's time to reap my reward," she gleefully responded.

I advised her, "Let's keep this as inconspicuous as we can to avoid any trouble. I've brought along someone to ensure our safety; he's waiting in my car, but once we leave the parking lot, you're on your own."

"Got it. After all these years, I think it's only right I get what I deserve."

"I agree, let's go."

We went into the bank and asked to see the Vice President, Mr. Bagwell, to gain access to the vault and the safe deposit boxes. As is the procedure, the bank has a key and the customer has another key to retrieve any contents. Once our box door was opened, Vice President Bagwell excused himself to allow us privacy.

Untouched for two years, we had to pull hard to remove the overloaded safe deposit box. We set the box on a nearby table and began quickly to unload the contents into Mary Rose's black rolling suitcase. There was a sealed envelope on top of the currency. She squealed with excitement as bundle after bundle of cash sporting a hundred dollar bill on top of the tightly wrapped cash bricks were stacked into the bag.

"I can't wait to get home and count all this cash. This day is going to change my life forever."

I peered through the glass doors as we prepared to leave. I thought it wise to scope out the parking lot for any nefarious activity. It was all I could do to hold Mary Rose back from just dashing out with her loot.

I saw her to her car, loaded her bag into the back seat at which she reprimanded me. "Oh no, I want that bag right here next to me in the passenger seat. It's mine, and I want to keep my eyes on it at all times and maybe reach over and pet it." She chuckled at her recent good fortune.

"Okay, well be careful. We should talk soon."

She couldn't resist a parting shot. "Oh yeah, one more thing, I really resented that Papa choose you as executor when I was the oldest surviving child after Vince's death, but that's over. Bye-Bye."

She gunned the engine of her fancy new black BMW and squealed out of the parking lot.

Now onto to the Security Bank to meet Dominic. Twenty minutes later, the scene was similar, but Dominic showed up with a shady looking sidekick.

"Dominic, whoever that is he cannot go into the bank with us. Can you not follow the simplest of directions?" I shouted.

"You probably don't realize it, but I'm your older brother, and I don't take orders from you," he angrily replied.

"The conditions of Dad's will are clear. We go in but your gorilla stays outside."

"Let's just get this over with, then I don't have to listen to you ever again *little* brother," Dominic gloated.

A repeat of the previous transaction at the first bank followed.

We slid the safety deposit box out. Another sealed envelope and bundles of cash had Dominic salivating and dropping bundles all over the floor in his greedy hast to stuff his inheritance into a duffle bag.

Wide-eyed, Dom couldn't resist saying, "After this, I don't need you. I don't need anybody!"

"Our father lived by the code that family is everything," I reminded him.

"He's gone. I don't to listen to him anymore. Ad I don't listen to you, ever again," he said smugly.

He ran out of the vault, but stopped at the door and glared at me as he left the building.

What a morning. I felt like I had just witnessed the worst display of disgusting greedy humanity ever. My father's words echoed in my ears, "Never reward bad behavior."

Even from the grave it seemed to me that he had sent that message.

Chapter XII

The Not so Big Surprise

Check that disgusting piece of business off the list. Now two thieving surviving siblings were awarded their inheritance. What I didn't expect was the next series of reactions. Within a matter of an hour both Mary Rose and Dom would call in a rage!

"You knew. You knew all the time!" Mary Rose screamed through the phone.

"Knew what? I have no idea what you're talking about."

"The evil trick Papa played on me; you were in on it," she yelled.

"I just followed the instructions according to our father's directions. I don't have a clue what you're talking about."

"I can assure you I'm going to contest this," she continued.

"I still don't know what's going on, but remember, it clearly stated in Papa's will anyone who contested the will in any way, or any part is, automatically out. You get zero."

Still enraged, Mary Rose continued, "What a rotten trick."

Confused still I merely said, "Trick?"

"All those wrapped bundles of cash had a hundred dollar bill on the top and the bottom with carefully cut blank paper in the center. Nothing more than a few thousand dollars when I was entitled to millions!"

"My phone is beeping; I have another call. Call me back in twenty minutes."

"Don't you hang up," she continued in desperation.

Click...

Switching over to call number two on the line was the cursing voice of Dominic. "You dirty bastard."

I could only think, *Oh, the irony.*

"Okay, so what's *your* problem?" hinting that I wasn't aware he had discovered his lottery bonus was actually the same fate as Mary Rose.

"I've been robbed, cheated out of my rightful inheritance."

"Okay, I just went through this with our sister, I have no idea what's going on."

"You knew. You and him were thick as thieves," he screamed.

"Interesting choice of words under the circumstances," I answered.

"So, *baby brother* what was the message in the envelope all about?"

"I saw an envelope in Mary Rose's safe deposit box and one in yours, I have no idea of the contents."

"When I opened it, in big bold letters it said, "NEVER REWARD BAD BEHAVIOR.""

"That's it?"

"Yeah, that's it."

"Hmm…that's interesting. Maybe you should examine your conscience, think about how that might apply to you." Thinking quickly, I started a little fishing expedition of my own to see if one of the culprits would bite. "Mary Rose already told me what you both did."

"That tramp, she said we should stick together and stay quiet about the money. It was all her idea. When I found out, I told her I'd keep my mouth shut for a piece of the action." He had just unwittingly confessed.

"Sorry, but it seems it's true, that saying, *no honor among thieves.* Look, my other line is ringing. I have to go."

Next call. "I want to know what the message inside the envelope means," said a still furious Mary Rose.

Shyly I asked, "What did it say?"

"Never reward bad behavior!" she yelled.

"Gee, I don't know. Think Mary Rose, do you have any idea what Papa might have meant by that?"

"Don't get cute with me. You probably have a pretty good idea of what happened. I'm sure big mouth Dominic told you already."

"He didn't tell me anything," I replied, trying not to laugh.

"All I know is the 80 bundles should have been eight hundred thousand dollars and the cute little top and bottom trick totals sixteen thousand dollars."

"Oh, wait—he did tell me that you two schemed together to help yourselves to a lot of cash from the business, and that it was your idea, and he blackmailed you into cutting him in."

"I knew it. I knew I couldn't trust him."

"Trust, under the current circumstances that seems like a strange word to throw around," I couldn't help but utter.

Surprise, surprise, but the surprises weren't over yet.

About a month later, just when it seemed the dust had settled, a knock at my door provided a new shocker. As if the previous disastrous inheritance distribution wasn't enough, I was in total disbelief at the appearance of Sister Angelina.

I looked through the peep hole in the door to see a vaguely familiar face, but Angelina was in street clothes instead of the religious habit she had worn for the last several years. She looked tanned, well rested, and full figured.

"Well, this is a surprise!"

She moved in for a hug then blurted out, "I've left the religious order. I just felt like the secular life was calling me back."

"What? After all these many years?" I asked.

Then the real reason surfaced.

"I want my share of our parent's money, the inheritance."

Stunned I replied, "I thought you understood that Papa was going to send a rather large sum of money to the facility you were serving at the time, I think it was St. Joseph's School. I know it was based strictly off your having taken a vow of poverty."

"I did, but now there's a change in plans. I became weary of a life of poverty," she responded.

"You'll have to contact your last location, St. Joseph's. That's where the money went. Ask them if it's retrievable. It was five hundred thousand dollars."

"I've already had the discussion, and they're not willing to give it back since it was designated to the school even though it was in my name."

"Well, that puts us in kind of an awkward position," I replied.

She continued, "It's my understanding that you got a large share of the cash and the house—that's pretty significant. From the looks of things, it appears that you are living the good life. Big house, nice cars, dressed well. Couldn't you let go of some of that money?" she asked.

"I'm certainly willing to help you out. How much do you think you would need?"

"Oh, let's say a couple of hundred thousand," She responded casually.

"Whew, that rolled off your lips pretty easily."

The religious life hadn't taken the edge off my previously rebellious sister as she cast the *if looks could kill* glance in my direction.

"Well, what can you do?" she pushed further.

"I think it would be fair to give you fifty thousand dollars to get started and make you a loan of another fifty thousand."

"That's the best you can do?" she angrily shouted.

Yep, that's the original version of a younger Angelina I remember! Bad girl gone good and good girl reverting back to bad.

"I'm afraid so. I have my life, my wife, and our family to consider also."

"What, and I'm not family? I guess I don't have much of a choice, maybe Mary Rose or Dominic can help me."

Boy was she ever in for a surprise!

Little did she know they were not very financially stable either. I wrote a check, Angelina angrily snatched it from my hand and turned away—no goodbye and certainly no thank you, and as soon as she backed her little SUV out of the driveway I called my bank to alert them about the transaction.

Maybe now all the ill-fated inheritance activity was behind me.

No such luck.

Not a week later another desperate call for money, this time it was Dominic. Prior to all this we hadn't spoken for months, so I knew this couldn't be good.

"Little brother I need your help." I could hear the genuine fear on his voice.

"Really, Dominic? I mean, really?"

"Please listen to me, please. I owe a lot of people a lot of money." His words carried the continued message of fright.

"Okay. How many is *a lot* of people, how much is *a lot* of money, and what is it for?" I felt like I already knew the answer to some of this.

"Tony, these are very bad people, I'm not kidding. I got myself in big trouble, the kind of trouble that could get me killed. Because of who these people are and my past I sure can't go to the police."

"Okay, slow down, and tell me exactly what's going on."

"It's complicated. I gambled with money I didn't have, bought drugs to resell and got screwed with bags of powdered dry wall instead of cocaine, and now these people have given me until the end of this week to come up with the money or else."

"It's unlikely they're going to kill you because then they'll never get, they're money. I learned the mob mentality from hanging around mobsters," I explained.

"Tony, you don't know these people, they'd kill me to send a message."

"Didn't you learn anything from Papa? These people won't come after you, they'll come after the closest people in your family. Us! If they kill you, they'd never get their money. So, how much do you need to get in the clear? Don't pad the number, tell me the real amount."

"I swear to God, the total is $34,000."

"Give me twenty-four hours to think about it. Call me back tomorrow."

"Please, I'm begging you, I'm scared," he desperately replied.

I already decide I would give him a loan for the money, but I also already knew I would never get it back, just like the *loan* to Angelina.

I told Catherine about the panicked phone call from Dominic, and in her true compassionate form she urged me to help him.

I spent a sleepless night worried that the bad guys might call in their marker early, but at 7 AM the phone rang, and it was Dom...obviously still alive.

"Hello."

"Please tell me you're going to help me out." The desperation in Dominic's voice was evident.

"I will—this time. But this is it, no more," I warned.

"I swear Tony, I'll change. I'll turn my life around. Thank you, thank you. How can I get the money?"

"You make arrangements to meet these people in a public place. Meet me at the St. Louis Metro bank at 9 AM, and just so you know I'm bringing two police detectives with me to ensure your safety and to make sure nothing goes wrong at either exchange. Set the time for the payoffs at noon, and my friends will stay with you the whole time. Call me when it's all done—and Dom, don't mess this up!"

Relieved, the voice on the other end of the phone replied, "I will, I mean, I won't... I mean... thank you, you're saving my life. I promise I'll do better; I'll change, I promise."

Time would tell.

For years I've said night prayers each evening at 9 PM. I remember those living and dead who have had an impact on me, and the hardest part is those who should have been loyal to me but went from family to foe. A life lesson for me was realizing as a normal human that the hardest thing to give is what you never received, patience, understanding, and unselfish love were all examples withheld in my life. In spite of what would have been my initial reaction, I continued to pray for Dominic and Mary Rose. I found it easier to visualize those I prayed for and seeing those faces each night allowed me to rekindle many of the best times. Several others just naturally earned a place on my list, like Oliver and his family which was composed of two stages. The first two children, Thomas and Caroline, reintroduced me to the fun of the little folks, later Chris and Kate came along.

Lessons came through awareness and deeper thought about interactions with children, especially our grandchildren. A prime example came years back when a four-year-old little Caroline aka *Cookie* and I were spending time together.

We made our way down the hall and into my office, I opened the closet where I kept a well-worn cardboard box. "All right, what do you want to play with?"

She walked over and dumps out the box and exclaimed, "Everything."

A sampling of the contents in the play box included a big ten-piece puzzle with, of course, only nine pieces visible. There was a bag of wooden blocks, the kind with numbers, letters, and farm animals on the faces. The blocks show evidence of use from many little hands—corners are worn off, some colors are faded, and cracks in the wood are proof that they've been used and abused. A box of crayons spilled out, broken, peeled, and some that are nothing more than nubs are scattered on the floor. The refrigerator door is already loaded with magnet connected juvenile art ripped from the coloring books

"What do you want to play with?" I asked, as we both assumed prone positions on the cool oak office floor.

"Let's color."

She grabbed the remnants of a red crayon and started to scribble across the face of a dog in the coloring book.

"Wait, you have to stay in the lines and pick a real color for the dog."

Cookie looked up, and with childhood innocence asked, "Why?"

"Well, that's the way it's supposed to be." I answered.

Again, she asked, "Why?"

"You know what, I'm not sure. Just do it the way you want to. You'll have plenty of rules to follow soon enough."

Satisfied with the answer she started the random red scribbling again.

As I reflected, a loud clap of thunder struck, and lighting flashed across the darkened sky. It startled her, and she jumped into my arms.

"I'm sacred, Poppy."

I held her close to comfort the little pajama-clad child. "It's okay. It's only a storm outside."

Her fright brought a tear to my own eyes, and as we stayed cheek to cheek, fear drops trickled from her eyes. I felt a single tear fall from my face and mingle with the tiny tears streaming down her chubby little cheek. I would do anything to protect this child, now I knew more than ever what my father meant when he said, "Family is everything." I now understood this innocent child and others who were not of my blood, were of my soul.

A flood of emotion came over me. It was like I could feel my father's presence in that very room at that very moment. At that moment, the previously ominous sky opened up, and the rays of the sun gradually turned the darkness back to daylight.

We looked out the office window, and I pointed and said to Cookie, "Look over there. Do you see that? It's a rainbow, that's God's promise that everything is going to be all right. Nothing in the world is powerful than a promise from God."

~

Months passed and there was no word from Dominic. I'd like to say I was surprised, but I wasn't. I actually took comfort in the thought that at least I had done the right thing and kept my word. My motivation often came from asking myself, *what would Papa do?* I did wonder about where Dom was and how he was getting by. My worry came from a compassion he didn't deserve. I viewed Dominic in the same category as coyotes and cockroaches—they seem to survive everything. I remained confident that he would seek shelter with me if things got ugly again, and that thought kept me on edge.

I'm not a fan of surprises, but you would think after this long I'd have gotten used to it. It seems there's always another surprise lurking around the corner.

Chapter XIII

The Memory Box

It was a stormy night complete with heavy rains and high winds plus the looming threat of a tornado.

We were settled in, and Catherine said, "Do you want me to microwave some popcorn?"

"Sure, I could do some popcorn. Don't forget, just two minutes ,otherwise it tastes burned."

"I can make popcorn dear!" she yelled back over her shoulder.

I took the heavy emphasis on *dear* as a caution to remain silent.

Little warning beeps came up as the dangerous weather warning message paraded across the bottom of the TV screen—bold letters proclaimed the intense storm system headed directly towards us.

Catherine and I had a specific foul weather plan, and when the warning sirens sounded, we were already huddled in our safe spot, a large walk in closet. You could hear the storm raging as we waited and nibbled on the freshly popped popcorn. Bottled water, popcorn, and the woman I love, I had all I needed. We both silently prayed for our safety and that of our neighbors. The lights flickered, and then we found ourselves completely engulfed in darkness. It's funny how quiet and eerie it gets when the electricity is out.

"Have you got your flashlight, Catherine?" I asked.

"Yes, the small one, but the batteries are weak. Wait here I'll be right back."

"Where would I go, I'd probably kill myself on the furniture—trip, fall, or who knows what."

"I'll be back," she said with a laugh.

My emergency plan is to count on Catherine. She knows where everything is stashed. She came back into the closet with one of those giant candles, and to catch the melting wax, one of our mismatched dessert plates. She noticed that I spread a comforter out on the floor of the closet thinking we might be there a while.

The candle was one of those Christmas gifts you get at parties, simple, inexpensive, and a candidate for regifting. She carefully pulled the clear wrap off of it. I noticed the label said, *pine forest*.

It had only a slight resemblance to a genuine pine smell but emitted more of a cheap imitation odor. The important thing was it would take us from the darkness to just enough light to illuminate the confines of our foul weather hideout.

She struck one of the strike anywhere matches, the popping sound followed by the familiar sulphur smell was a boyhood reminder of when my father would light a match out of one of those paper matchbooks to fire up one of his unfiltered Lucky Strike cigarettes.

As we waited out the storm, boredom coupled with a modicum of fear set in. We were clad in our traditional sleep clothes—I was wearing red and black plaid fleece sleep pants, and she was in a faded flannel night gown. Foolishly I thought, *I hope nothing bad happens. I'd hate for us to be found looking like this.*

Catherine asked innocently, "I've often wondered about that wooden box there on your shelf."

"Wondered?"

"Yes, what's in it?"

"The box itself is a great story. I love the smell of cedar and saw it while we were on a vacation trip to Michigan. The tag description on the shelf said it was made from locally harvested cedar. I asked my father if I could have it as a souvenir of our trip, and he acknowledged my request begrudgingly with a simple affirmative nod. I pulled it down and handed it to him so we could pay for it on the way out of the store. Once we got into the car, I couldn't resist flipping it open to smell that pleasant cedar smell. The box was equipped with a small hasp, and I knew there was a tiny lock at home that would secure the contents from the prying eyes and hands of my unscrupulous siblings."

"Good story, but what's in it?"

"I don't know where the key is now, it's been years since I opened it, but I think I can pry the lock open if you're really interested."

"Sure, I'd like to see what's in it. It's not like we have anything else to do," she said.

I grabbed small multi-tool from my shelf and easily popped the cheap tiny lock open.

"There we go. Wow, it's been forever since I looked at this stuff. I barely remember what all is in here."

I dumped the contents out recklessly with little regard for the treasured memories that came spilling out. Immediately I noticed the aromatic cedar smell was almost gone.

Metallic sounds came from coins and keys.

"What's this coin? It looks foreign?" Catherine asked.

"Oh, I'd forgotten about that. It's a Canadian dollar. They call them "loonies" because there's a loon on one side—it's the Canadian national bird—I got that coin in change when we were on a fishing trip in Canada. I still recall the sound of those loons when the days were winding down. When we graduated eighth grade, my father would let us each pick a place to go. I chose Canada. I really think he did that for us because he didn't think any of us would ever graduate anything more than grade school," I said with a chuckle. "We fished, ate our catch around a campfire, watched the moon come up and the stars appear—millions of them lit up the night sky. The owls hooted, and each night a gentle breeze fanned the last of the flames from our campfire."

"Wow, that's quite a picture you just painted."

I smiled at the compliment.

Next question from Catherine, "What about these other coins?"

"Now you're going to really think I'm weird. That's what I call *perfect change.* There's a quarter, a dime, a nickel and a penny, one of everything."

"So, what's the significance of *perfect change?*"

"On our first date, I was paying for our meal, and the bill was $24.59. I gave the cashier a twenty dollar bill and a five, the change was exactly 41 cents, a quarter, a dime, a nickel, and a penny. When I was emptying pockets that night I thought to myself, it was perfect change, for a perfect night—with a perfect girl."

"Awwww!" she said as she leaned over and kissed me on the side of my face. "How about this feather? It looks like it changes color in the candle light."

"I know, isn't that cool? Long ago a lady friend of mine, Lynne, was going to South America to do a habitat study on the Amazon River, you know that *other* Amazon." I paused to allow time for the dramatic effect of a bad joke.

After an eye roll, she asked, "So, what else about the feather?"

"She brought it back to me all the way from the Amazon—it's a parrot feather. Watch this." I turned it slowly and even in the dim candlelight it did changed colors from yellow to red, then to blue when I rolled it slowly between my fingers. It was as if it possessed some mystical, magical qualities.

"We're you romantically involved?" asked the inquisitive Catherine.

"Oh no, she literally was just a friend. She was out of my league, but I loved that she thought enough of me to bring the feather all the way back to the states."

"She was *crushing on you*, you just didn't know it," Catherine remarked.

"Maybe, but you know me—I don't pick up on subtlety. You have to hit me right between the eyes with it," I responded, laughing.

"What about this little black leather coin purse?"

"That's really special, it's one of the few things that survived through many years. It belonged to my paternal grandmother

Rosa. She died in her mid-thirties, and Grandpa Vincent got rid of almost everything of hers. I found it in tucked away in an old shoe box, on a closet shelf, in what was a much smaller closet than this. It still has her rosary in it."

The once supple leather was cracking with age, but I knew her hands had opened and closed it lovingly during her short time on earth. I imagined her fingers traveling the rosary beads in times of fear, faith, desperation, pain, or maybe even in thanksgiving.

Another of the artifacts that gave off the metallic sound was one of those old-school key rings.

Catherine commented, "Whose keys?"

"Those were my father's, while everybody fought over the items deemed more expensive, I wanted personal things. A simple metal ring with three keys, one for the front door of the restaurant, the second a house key, and the last one his car key. These were the things vital and important to my father. I think the keys say a lot about him. To me, the fact that he carried these every day meant more than most other items."

"You are so much deeper than most people realize."

Quickly deflecting, I asked, "You might have never noticed, but Samurai's collar tag is on my key ring. I never referred to the pets as dogs, to me they were family."

"Hey, look at this," she continued. "Here's a flower petal pressed between two pieces of tape. This has got to be old; the tape has turned yellow."

I felt a lump in my throat as I explained, "That came from my mother's funeral. She was eventually cremated, and at her celebration of life I pulled a rose from one of the wreaths. She was so special; she really had a tough life. Maybe this rose petal deserves a better place of honor, but I really did cherish the items contained in the box."

I think Catherine sensed my pain and moved on quickly. "What about these, I think they're car keys?"

"My first new car—that's when there was an ignition key and

a trunk key—it was a 1969 Camaro, red with a 327 engine. At the time it cost $2300!"

"That was your first car? Wow!"

"No, my first *new* car. My first car was a 1961 Chevy station wagon with 241,000 miles on it. It broke down every other week and once had two flat tires at the same time. The transmission went out when I was driving up a steep hill, and I was out of control going backwards at about 35 miles an hour. The rear seat of the that station wagon folded down making it the perfect vehicle for the drive-in movies, a Friday night ritual. Good Times!"

"Please no more details. Okay, how about this pocketknife. What's this about, and how do you remember all this stuff down to the smallest detail?" she wondered.

"I remember what's important to me. That pocketknife belonged to my maternal grandfather, Farantello. He kept it on his dresser and each morning would put it in his pocket. My grandmother had a little blown glass wishing well complete with a blown glass bucket on the same dresser. I remember my grandparents' house, it always seemed to smell old and stale, plus the closets reeked of moth balls. Still lots of good memories, good food for every meal, playing with their dog, Prince, and each visit later in the evening included card games at the big wooden kitchen table. After all us kids were shooed away, banished to another part of the house, I'd sneak back and peek through the doorway and listen and watch as they dealt hands of poker, stacked their red, white, and blue poker chips, and cursed in Italian when their luck was bad. In our family the first Italian words you learned were the cuss words."

I laughed as Catherine displayed a look of disgust knowing it was probably true.

Seeing a black velvet ribbon threaded through a red glass bead, I quickly scooted it under several of the other items. For now, the story behind this item was best left unsaid.

"And about this?" She was holding a broken Indian arrowhead.

"I found that alongside a creek. I held it trying to imagine how it was made thinking it was hundreds of years ago, as I got older, I realized it was more likely thousands of years ago. I kept it because it provided a sobering thought that there were a lot of people that came before me, gone now. For years I looked for more Indian artifacts, but this was the only one I have found. Even if it's broken it's special to me, if nothing else it's a reminder of simpler times."

"Did anyone else see your little collection?"

"No, they wouldn't have understood, none of them—and my father would have laughed, deeming all this as worthless junk. Maybe he would have appreciated the family related items but surely not the rest. I feel a real connection to all the people that held these things in their hands."

My voice cracked temporarily overcome by emotion as I searched for the appropriate words to describe my attachment and deep connection to these personal treasures to my people and the past.

"Admittedly, I live in my own strange little world, and my world is small. I like it that way."

Catherine looked lovingly at me, tiny tears welling up in her eyes, and said, "I don't think it's strange."

Sensing my vulnerability, she quickly asked, "How about this little gold cross, what's its significance?"

"I wore that for years, the chain broke, and I never replaced it. It's tarnished, and on the back, it says *Italy*, I just couldn't toss it out. The cross had been traditionally blessed by a parish priest; I always felt safe when I was wearing it."

Now the imitation pine smell of the burning candle was more evident. "This was kind of fun. I'm glad the power went out. I have to tell you your flannel nightgown makes you look gorgeous in that candlelight. It's simple and soft, beautiful but even more delicate and inviting, just like you."

Without saying a word, she gently slid her gown over her head, revealing her full self, the natural candle light added a romantic glow to her body image. Then she reached over and gently pulled the knot on the drawstring of my sleep pants guiding them down my legs, then took my hand as she brushed aside all the little treasures from the wooden cedar memory box. At that moment, to me it felt like we were the only two people in the world. We made the most sensual, passionate love ever. It turned into another treasured memory.

The storm had long since passed, but we barely noticed as we had been deeply occupied in the explanations contained by the contents of the ancient box. We were exhausted now and drifted off to a peaceful sleep only to awaken a while later by the jolt of multiple household appliances starting up in unison—sounds indicating the return of the electricity.

Life, at least for now, was good.

Chapter XIV

Family Triumphs and Troubles

Life—sometimes it's good, sometimes it's bad, and sometimes it's terrible, at least it is for me. There's not a lot of in between. No family is immune from trouble, and our family certainly was no exception. We sure had our share of trouble, plus some. There was, however, plenty to celebrate. Each day brought a new adventure, family affairs, business, outdoor activities like an unplanned fishing trip, spontaneous day time dates, or precious moments just sitting in a backyard swing feeling the breeze, watching birds or lightning bugs, or imagining cloud formations as being anything we might imagine—each of these special in their own way.

Today schedule amounted to a quick trip into the city for my annual physical. Routine stuff. I could already hear Dr. Stewart; "Okay, Tony blood pressure a little high, cholesterol probably good and (clearing of the throat accompanied by the phrase) you could stand to lose about ten pounds."

"I knew you were going to say that. I'm Italian Doc. We don't eat because were hungry; we eat because it tastes good."

"Well, I practice what I preach, maybe you noticed I lost fifteen pounds."

"Yeah, maybe you noticed, I found it." I was amused. Him, not so much.

"While you're here let's run a stress test and do an EKG."

"Stress test, I didn't know there was going to be a quiz!" My second attempt at humor was met with silence.

Whisked off to another chilly examination room where all kinds of high-tech equipment lined the walls, I sat and waited and waited.

When the doctor came in this time he was accompanied by an attractive nurse.

She asked me to take my shirt off so she could attach electrodes to me. She shaved patches of hair off my chest before attaching the electrodes.

Noting her shy demeanor, I broke the ice by saying, "If we were in Italy this would mean we're engaged."

Three people in the room and I was the only one laughing.

After the completion the EKG, I received my next set of instructions.

"Okay, let's hop on the treadmill."

I avoided verbalizing the multiple obvious openings to sarcasm as I stepped on the rubber matted in-motion treadmill.

I kept pace with the brisk flow of the humming machine, as Doctor Stewart placed his stethoscope on my chest and for a few minutes moved it around strategically.

Taking his clipboard, the doctor scribbled notes feverishly and advised, "You can put your shirt back on. I'll be right back."

The nurse left, and I was seated impatiently on an examining table anxious to get on with my day.

After a few minutes the doctor returned with a somber look on his face. "I don't mince words, you have a serious blockage to your heart."

"What? I feel great. Are you sure."

He replied with a stern look, "We need to run some tests tomorrow, a coronary angiogram. I'll be inserting a thin tube into your artery, the one in the leg, then guide it to the heart, a dye is injected through the catheter, which allows the arteries to be seen on X-ray. Then I'll determine if coronary artery disease is present and if treatment like angioplasty or bypass surgery is necessary.

"You have to be kidding, I have plans to go out of town," I protested.

"If you were my brother, I'd advise you to do the very same thing…today; no later than tomorrow!"

"You're serious?"

"Very serious. I'll set it up, see you tomorrow. Be at the hospital at 6 AM."

How was I going to tell Catherine? No more guilt from hiding information. As I walked through the door, Catherine was relaxed and reading one of her romance novels.

She casually asked, "How did it go?"

"It could have been better," I said.

"Did the doctor give you grief about your weight?"

"No, well kind of, but there's more…now don't get excited."

"Why, what's wrong?" she inquired in a panicked tone.

"He ran some tests and thinks I have a blockage in my heart. I feel okay, but he insists that I go to the hospital tomorrow morning early for an angiogram. Do you know what that is?"

"Yes, I know," she said with a high degree of worry coupled with frustration at the question.

"It'll all be fine. I'm telling you I feel great," I confidently exclaimed. I tried to think of a witty comment to lighten the mood, but generally that just brings out a zero level of tolerance.

"I'm scared!" she allowed.

"Don't be. I promise, it's going to be okay."

Neither of us slept well. We repeatedly checked in with each other through the night.

"Tony, are you sleeping?"

"No."

"What if—"

I immediately interrupted Catherine question of concern. "I don't do *what ifs*."

"I can't help but worry."

"I know. If it were you, I would worry, but I really believe it will be okay. Remember when we pray the Lord's prayer together, "Thy will be done?" We both have that kind of faith."

Silently I went through the various scenarios if it in fact wasn't fine. I had verbalized to Catherine many times that she was too nice and tolerated too much from people and the world around her. My normal comment was that it was my lot in life to be the voice for those who wouldn't speak up and to stand up for those who wouldn't or couldn't defend themselves.

With the arrival of morning, I realized this was a *no breakfast"* start to my day. I calmed myself by thinking of all the junk food I could eat after the tests were run.

Already knowing the answer, I still felt obliged to ask Catherine, "Are you going to eat anything?"

"I'm too nervous to eat."

"Okay. In that case let's just get an early start to the hospital. I'm sure there'll be a lot of paper work to fill out."

The drive was quiet with a tension unusual for us.

As we walked through the self-opening door, immediately that hospital medicine smell hit me and formed a knot in my stomach.

I sat down in the row of chairs, and Catherine took control. She approached the admissions station and began the barrage of questions and answers that are all part of the program.

Catherine navigated through the process which seemed like questions that would never end. She returned and took a seat next to me and presented me with paperwork to sign. Lots of words serving as essentially a disclaimer relieving the hospital, doctors, and anyone associated from any potential responsibility in the event of a problem.

Just as I began to mildly protest a nurse popped out of a door explaining, "We're ready for you now Mr. LeoMorte."

A quick kiss and a rushed *I love you* to reassure Catherine had me trailing behind the nurse to a small closed curtain area.

The nurse routinely announced, "If you'll change into that hospital gown I'll come back and prep you for the procedure."

Prepping me for the procedure, I imagined, would amount to hoisting my gown and someone giving me an embarrassing buzz cut. *Ugh!*

Moments later I was modeling a flimsy excuse for a covering and sporting a fresh trim. Soon, my doctor entered.

"Good morning Tony! So, here's what's going to happen, we'll wheel you in, insert a tube in your groin and inject you with a dye that can be seen on something resembling a TV screen."

Cold, apprehensive and with my rear end hanging out, I was at a loss for a witty comeback.

Dr. Stewart continued, "You'll be awake the whole time and can see as the dye flows toward your heart. This is a routine procedure, and we'll know a lot more in the next hour or so."

"If you find something, will you make a diagnosis and do the necessary steps to patch me up today?" I asked.

"I can't know that until we determine the amount of blockage," was his response.

Strange—when you're in a foreign environment, you notice things that would blend in otherwise. I scanned the room nervously, the floors gleaming, probably freshly waxed, I noticed the ceiling tiles had evidence of the slightest water drip likely coming from the roof, the walls were bare with one exception, a crucifix near the door.

I couldn't help but think of poor Catherine out there in the waiting area, worried, not knowing what was happening and what the test would show. I had to admit that I too had serious concerns as I whispered a prayer for a positive outcome.

Dr. Stewart recognized my semi silent uttering of the Our Father and said, "I too am a man of faith. Let's pray together."

Those few words encourage me toward the belief that God's hand would guide me through this.

"Are you ready? I'll get someone to wheel you in."

My gurney pilot navigated through a corridor maze. Much like a bad shopping cart, my gurney had one of those damaged, irregular wobbling wheels—it actually made me smile. I soon found myself in a small confined area devoid of anything but a few cabinets, a table with a few items to be used in the test, and a TV screen on a long adjustable arm. The area I was in now seemed noticeably colder than the other parts of the hospital.

A local anesthesia numbed me, and the tube was inserted, a slight pinch but barely noticeable. I could feel the injection of the dye—it was warm—and true to Dr. Stewarts word, I could see the path of the dye coursing through my veins.

"Are you okay?" he asked.

Putting on my bravest smile, I responded, "I tolerate pain well, I got a lot of practice in my first marriage." Then I added, "Yeah, I'm fine, I just want to make sure you're okay."

"Do you ever stop cracking jokes?"

I invoked my right to remain silent.

He stopped speaking and stared intently at the TV screen. He watched it, and I watched him looking for a reaction.

Without a word he turned away, and when he came back, he had two more doctors with him.

They huddled up for a brief consultation, looked at the screen together, grave looks came over their faces. They walked about five feet, lowered their surgical masks and continued in hushed tones.

I could only think things weren't looking good.

Dr. Stewart walked toward me and leaned over, "I don't know how to tell you this…but whatever was there yesterday is not there today."

"What does that mean?" I asked in a voice of concern.

"The blockage I saw yesterday is gone!"

"Are you sure?

"I've never seen anything like this," he said in amazement.

"Hmmm… I'm too mean for a miracle, and you're too good a doctor for a misdiagnosis."

"I can't explain it."

"Let's chalk it up to the power of prayer," I said with a smile.

For a few moments we just looked at each other in a stunned silence. The nurse volunteered to go into the waiting area and advise Catherine that the testing was complete and that the doctor would be out momentarily to speak with her. In a few minutes Dr. Stewart walked towards Catherine in the waiting area, she jumped up and met him halfway across the room.

"Mrs. LeoMorte, Tony did well."

Catherine interrupted the doctor with the panicked question, "Did well, what does that mean? What treatment is next for him?"

"I'd say a hearty breakfast followed by a nap. I'll let him tell you himself about the miraculous results. We'll get him into a room and come get you."

I was required to spend some time in the recovery room, and for me the room lit up when Catherine walked in flashing a giant smile of relief. She leaned over the bed and gave me a huge hug, tears of joy escaped her eyes and landed on my pillow.

With reassurance I said, "I'm fine. God has once again blessed me. They discovered there's no heart blockage. We can go home in a little while. I just have to be careful not to start bleeding from the artery where they inserted the tube."

"I'm so glad you're okay. I bet you want to get home and get something to eat."

"They said they could bring me breakfast. But hospital food? Yuk!"

"I'll make you a big breakfast, everything you like once we get home."

A few hours later I was delivered to the curb in a wheelchair at their insistence, and they helped me in to the car for what would be a welcome relief—a ride home.

After a previous diagnosis of cancer and now this; it was undeniable that the Lord was watching over me. Two health scares and two dodges from disaster.

I felt invincible.

It seemed there was the never-ending threat of *the curse*. According to the dream and story related to me, it was supposed to last one hundred years—if you believe in those sorts of things.

Even though we were decades past the hundred-year mark, it appeared there was no escape. Was this just my destiny?

Admittedly, at times there was a sadness for the lack of family interaction, fueled most likely by pleasant memories of the innocence of days gone by. There were the things we laughed at as kids, the unfounded fears we found exciting once we became accustomed to it stemming from being the offspring of people with dangerous connections, and then there was the simplicity of those times. Technology hadn't invaded the world, innovations were limited. My life was better when it was routine and predictable. I yearned for simplicity.

Still the recurring thoughts so engrained in my head were my father's words, "Family is everything!" Was he right, or was that an outdated concept that died with him and the old timers? Vince's violent death pushed us all further apart. We drifted into our own little worlds. Now with both parents gone, the glue that kept is together had allowed jealousy and animosity to creep in and shatter the family unit that was so European. The early competition for our parent's approval seemed to be a catalyst for discontent among all of our family members. Money was a false measure of success and did little to quiet the competitive chaos among the remaining family members.

New found wealth in hand, Angelina rushed into an ill-advised marriage. She had been shielded for years, sequestered from the real world in the religious life, and now she spent money like a drunken sailor.

I tried to give her fatherly advice. "Can't you just wait? What's your hurry? Remember, that money won't last forever?"

She responded like a teenager. "I spent years of my life dedicated to the happiness of others. It's my turn."

"This outside world is different now. Dominic is proof that the world we live in today doesn't tolerate foolishness." I tried to convince her.

"Foolishness? It's my turn to be happy," she responded angrily.

"You could be just as happy in a year or two. Be patient."

"My whole adult life I've had people telling what to do, where I could go, what to eat, and even what I could wear. I had no money of my own."

Frustrated I said, "That's exactly my point. Ease into this life, take your time."

"Time is ticking. I've had my happiness delayed long enough," she responded

"Okay, let me tell you how the story ends. You hurry to the altar, this guy isn't the prince charming you think he is, you go through your money, and he waves as he goes out the door."

"Ridiculous. I know what I'm doing. I don't need your advice or your approval."

The old adage, *time will tell,* was never more accurate. When the money was gone, so was he. I never thought "I told you so" were welcomed words, so I refrained in hopes of at least salvaging this familial relationship.

Peace was all I wanted. Would I ever have it?

Chapter XV

Good Times

Old memories are fine, but I found making new memories even better. As we aged, or *matured* we jokingly said, we found new joy in old things but also stepped out of our comfort zone occasionally.

"You can't open new doors with old keys," Catherine said.

We had mastered the skill of looking at things like we were seeing them for the first time—or like we were looking at them for the last time. Simple pleasures and the joy that comes with finding the right person were our constant companions each day. We hit a few little bumps in the road, but for the most part we had a relationship that was the envy of most of the people who knew us. I liked to believe I summed it up best in the wedding vows I wrote.

Older people are cool because we know all of life's secrets, we lived them, and we learned them.

We know marriage and any relationship is NOT 50/50 because that would mean you're measuring.

We know time is precious because we have more days behind us than we do in ahead of us.

We know we have more money but less time and know to use both of them wisely.

We know you can fall in love over and over again with the same person.

We know the value of a handwritten note, one picked wild flower or that smile that silently says, "I understand," also that our favorite music is the other persons laugh.

We know to pray not for what we want but what we've had and pray before we sleep, eat, or play.

We understand it's great to know Psalm 23, John 3:16 or to use Corinthians Chapter 13, we know it's great to know the Bible and even greater to live the Bible ... and that why we're here.

The pastor performing our ceremony was moved to tears as he read the words to those in attendance. This was the start to something special.

One day as I walked past the shelf in my closet, I felt a sense of guilt and was haunted by the lack of complete honesty with Catherine regarding one of the items in my cedar memory box—the black velvet ribbon. The story would require a kind of an embarrassing confession, and I wasn't ready to divulge details.

When I was recently divorced, I often ventured out following my feelings of independence. On a traditional fishing trip to Blue Springs State Park, I was trout fishing. For years I went on the opening day of trout season. On my second day there, I watched a young woman wading the stream. We exchanged glances, and my eyes followed her as she moved further downstream. Her technique with the fly rod gave every indication that she was not very experienced. It seemed most of her casts were stuck in the lower branches of creekside trees, on the bottom of the stream or everywhere but in potential trout water.

She smiled and announced, "I'm really not very good at this."

I replied, "Nope, you're not. Can I show you?" I anxiously offered.

"Oh, would you?"

I stepped closer and avoided the awkward handshake. "I'm Tony."

"Hi, I'm Amy."

"The key is to let the equipment do the work. Trust the feeling and the rod, let the line lay out behind you before you try to start it forward. It's a common mistake," I advised.

Her first attempt after the instructions was still off. I slyly took the opportunity to move in behind her with reverse hug and say, "Let me show you. Do you mind?"

Not waiting for a response, I wrapped my hands over her wrists; we started the back cast and then when the timing was right pushed the fly rod forward, the line shot through the guides, sprayed excess water off and traveled smoothly toward the target area.

"There you go, perfect."

She smiled. "Oh, you're right. That's much better. You're a good teacher."

"It just takes practice and then the fish catching is a lot easier. I'll let you get back to fishing now."

"Don't go. I could use your help," She pleaded.

I thought, *She's cute; probably at least ten years younger than me.* After scoping her out closely I saw no visible tan lines on her left-hand ring finger that would indicate marriage. *What the heck.*

Just when it seemed things were going well, the rain started. We looked at each other and laughed.

"It looks like the rain is settling in. I guess that's it for a little while."

She looked disappointed and offered, "My cabin is close by. Do you want to wait out the rain there?"

"Which cabin is yours?" I asked.

"They only had the big lodge cabin open, so I took it. It's larger than I wanted and certainly more than I needed, but I took it anyway."

The cabin I had reserved was described as rustic. In my experience that usually meant an uncomfortable bed and a Bible, with the uninvited companionship of a few mice and spiders.

I happily obliged. "Your cabin is closer; we can go there. I've never been in the lodge cabin. I bet it's nicer than mine."

I took the rods in one hand and instinctively grabbed her

hand with my other. We jogged up the slippery hill, giggling, and made it just in time to avoid the arrival of a heavy downpour.

This cabin was nice. At the entrance of her lodge cabin was a small gravel parking area, and a compact car was parked in front of the doorway, I assumed it was hers. It had Missouri plates and a Hertz rental sticker on the back window.

The door hinges squeaked announcing our entrance. As we opened the unlocked door, we were greeted by the musty smell you might expect from an old fishing shelter. It was certainly aged. The pine floors gave slightly with each step, a scan of the room revealed it was equipped with an ancient hand-hewn log double bed, the night stand next to the bed had the customary Gideon Bible, a black rotary phone, a local yellow pages phone book, and an old-time radio. The centerpiece of the lodge was a large floor to ceiling fieldstone fireplace complete with a randomly stacked supply of seasoned firewood. At the end of the room there was a rickety looking wooden table with a few apples, a bag of chips, a couple of cans of Vienna sausages, and crackers scattered across it.

Amy suggested we pull off our shoes and get rid of the wet outer wear. We did the one-legged hop to get rid of the wet boots and discarded water-soaked jackets, hats, and fishing vests on the floor.

The rain slowed, and the metal roof played the soft music most country people can identify with.

"Should we make a fire in the fireplace?" Amy asked.

"I can. Does that mean you're giving up on the trout for the rest of the day?"

"I think so," she responded sadly.

With the help of some old newspapers, some little twigs for fire starter, and some carefully assembled logs there was soon a roaring fire, the room took on a totally different atmosphere, cozy, and except for the intermittent popping sounds of the burning wood, peaceful with a sense of relief from the outside weather and world.

Amy looked at me. With the flames from the fire illuminating the room, she asked the one-word question, "Married?"

"No ma'am, divorced. You?"

"Free as a bird," she tweeted happily.

Almost as if in a fantasy, she moved closer to me. She seemed to float as she closed the distance between us, then put her hand on the back of my neck, drew me closer, and stepped up on her tip toes and kissed me like I hadn't been kissed in a while.

Without a word she took control, she pulled the tattered quilt from the bed and meticulously spread it, almost like a couple preparing for a picnic, she was careful to place it a safe distance from the fireplace and the popping embers. Then this little temptress stood up and guided me over to the center of the patchwork quilt.

The soft light now danced off the walls of the room and reflected in her eyes; she began to slowly disrobe tossing the rest of her clothes into a pile on the floor. Curiously she had a black velvet ribbon fastened around her neck that she decided to leave on. The wide ribbon was slightly drawn together in the center by a single red glass bead.

New to this type of unanticipated attention, I asked, "Are you sure you want to do this?" Even though I was questioning this, I was hoping she would say yes.

She merely nodded her head.

Trying not to stare, I scanned her taut body—no piercings, no tattoos, she was toned like a healthy young woman, like an athlete or dancer would be. She had the face of a model, with ice blue eyes, long light brown hair complete with red high-lights—she resembled a mythical princess. Her lips turned up slightly at the corners of her mouth giving her an impish grin. She didn't merely move though, she seemed to glide as she stepped closer to me.

Soon we were facing in a full embrace. This was a drastically different experience for me, completely out of character, but after a long period of unintended abstinence, it sure felt good. We enjoyed each other into exhaustion, feel asleep in an embrace, woke in the middle of the night, and again found pleasure in each other.

The next day after sufficient wake up time, we shared the feeling almost like a honeymoon couple, we traveled down the road to small country store to stock up on eggs, bread, and a few necessary items. Other than that, we never left the cabin. After a quick breakfast Amy, in a whisper said, "I'm going for a walk in the woods, sit outside or along the banks of the stream."

"Wait, I'll go with you," I commented.

Each time she ventured out in an innocence that belied the worldly process, she would ask, "Can I go alone? I don't often get time to myself. I won't be gone long."

"Sure, I can catch up on my sleep." *And regain my strength*, I thought.

I watched through the window as she left, stepped off the wrap-around porch, and strolled out into the grass. She stopped and sat down Indian style and just stared at the water. The gentle breeze moved her hair around slowly, seductively, and the sun accentuated the highlights in her waist length chestnut hair.

I took a moment to further familiarize myself with the room. On a small table on the other side of the bed sat a few books. The *Insects of the World, European History*, and *A Woman's Guide to Independence—Odd reading material*, I thought. *Bugs, history and an instruction on becoming an independent woman.*

To further add to the mystery, in conversations I initiated, she would give trite answers, her responses, "I'm dull, there's really not much to tell" or turn the attention towards me.

I pressed a little more, "What's the fascination about entomology?"

She smiled. "Oh you know about the study of insects?"

I countered with, "Only because I swat flies, squash spiders, and imitate Mayflies when trout fishing. My expertise is limited."

Once again, a deflection as she proclaimed, "I have varied

interests, I like to learn as much as I can about places and even more about people."

While I thought it strange, it merely added to the intrigue, I got to know her body very well but not her brain or personal background.

Our clothes had dried sufficiently on the shower curtain rod and in between love making sessions we slept in the log-frame bed on a mattress that sunk in toward the middle conveniently pushing us closer together through the night. The setting of the sun, morning sunrises, nature sounds, and fireplace flames were ideal, couple that in the evenings with a full moon, and the acoustical accompaniment of the occasional owl hoot, chirping crickets, and the sound of the flowing stream—the combination was heavenly.

Lost in lust, I still knew very little about Amy. She had more energy than me, and while I spent time napping, exhausted by her sexual enthusiasm, she continued to take her brief strolls, always solo, exploring the natural surroundings. She seemed pensive and preoccupied. We spent a great deal of our waking time in silence feeling no need for mindless conversation. She sometimes just paged through her reading material. I did find it odd that even when we showered, she never removed the velvet choker with the single red bead.

On the third morning, after another long night of passion, I woke up... and mysteriously she was gone.

Oddly enough her velvet ribbon was left on the table, the red bead shown brilliantly in the sunlight. No note, no goodbye, the car and she had somehow silently disappeared.

It suddenly hit me, I didn't even know her last name, where she lived, or what she did. Was this all a dream? I couldn't help but wonder if these uncharacteristically wild days would come back to haunt me. Maybe it was remorse for such guilty pleasure.

As I left to go my cabin, I pocketed the velvet ribbon as a reminder of this strange, incredibly wild, unpredictable but memorable time. The black velvet choker with its singular bright red bead made its way into the memory box, tucked away where it resided untouched, but not forgotten for years.

Did I dare tell this story to Catherine? How would she feel? If I hadn't lived it and someone told me the story, I'm not sure I would believe it. Looking back, it seemed so irresponsible, so unlike me.

While we had settled into a routine life, Catherine had the urge to travel. I had to be coaxed to even try new food, I was such a creature of habit. We talked, schemed, and dreamed about far away places, but it seemed like what should be a slow-paced life often turned hectic. While she spoke of it sparingly, I knew it was always in the back of Catherine's mind.

I believed I like the routine life because of the lack of pre-dictability of my early years and the losses I suffered in family or my failed marriage. Unfortunately, this made me predictble, which is not viewed as a good quality by people with the Italian mob mentality.

Catherine and I were well matched—she was optimistic, I was more pessimistic (I viewed it as realistic); she was refined, I was rough around the edges. This went way beyond being able to finish each other's sentences, I knew what to expect and used that to try to make life better. I always believed you didn't have to live it to learn it, and the best lessons were those that I could view as a spectator and not suffer the consequences of poor life-altering choices. Age and experience are of great value.

The basis of our solid marriage was a genuine sharing of core values. She trusted me, and I trusted her, we communicated often and well. While our backgrounds were vastly different, we, in every way, made a good team. Some might view us as boring. I saw it as secure. Our choice of friends was different. My choice of friends mirrored my early interest in fishing, martial arts, and American history. Catherine gravitated towards educated, refined people. One long-time friend came from as far back as high school, John Blakemore; another from a previous work place experience, Ron McCarthy. We corresponded infrequently but managed to pick up where we left off when we got together. We were all like old shoes, not much to look at but comfortable. I didn't need a lot of friends, just the good reliable ones. We shared very little in the way of expectations, but we all took what the relationships had to offer.

Lots of people shunned the LeoMorte's because of the infamous last name. Some in the community avoided us and referred to us as those *I-talian* gangsters. There were a few couples whose company Catherine and I enjoyed—Norman and Shelly Burns, Tommy and Bea Evers, along with Mike and Judith Vinateri were people whose company we treasured. There were gatherings at local restaurants because the guys liked to eat, and the women enjoyed some non-testosterone kind of conversations, plus there would be no cooking and clean up. Even though there was some age disparity we got along well. Catherine and I offered wisdom only life experiences could give, the Burns' had business and school backgrounds, and the Evers were talented in many other ways. Tommy could build or fix anything, and Bea was a world-class photographer and skilled in crafts. The Vinateris were kind and the most grounded of the group, generous with their time and talents.

Sometimes a few of us even fished together, genuine proof of our admiration for each other, we went out for Friday movies or sat and talked about current affairs or the demise of the world we all once knew. As these relationships grew, we felt more comfortable about discussing family, successes, and failures. Between us there were technical skills, mechanical aptitude, outdoor interests, and the fun of sharing family stories. We were comfortable enough to lower our guards and laugh, talk, and openly express opinions without fear of judgment. None of us were drinkers, but the ability to laugh at past experiences or share real life hopes and fears drew us all closer over time. I had always been wary of letting my guard down, but these folks seemed genuine. It was refreshing to laugh again. Our circle of friends was small which left a lot of time for family. When your circle is small you can give a lot of attention to those people whose presence you cherish. It allows for more time and an intimacy lost in larger groups.

Sometimes friends turned into family. Family, the true meaning of it, at least for me, seemed to constantly shift through the course of my life.

Chapter XVI

Travel Plans

When diversity in life opportunities exist, you dive in, and for the LeoMorte family, at least for Catherine and me, one of those opportunities was travel. I had traveled extensively and was jaded as to the enjoyment of new cities and old hotel rooms. Catherine had been limited in her travels, but it was predictable that her wanderlust would resurface from time to time. I knew eventually I would acquiesce, and we would have to pack up and add new adventures to our life resume.

We frequently enjoyed local day trips, destinations were normally close to home and pretty tame. It may be a park, the zoo, a new restaurant or just an exploratory drive to scope out a new fishing spot. After traveling for business, I came to despise the routine, the airport foul ups, delays, gate changes, snarled out of town traffic, the hotel food, and the whole idea of business on the road. Once a requirement, now I only wanted to travel for my own enjoyment. Catherine yearned for what she thought would be long distance adventures.

One day, while watching an outdoor show, we spotted a possible adventure to a wilderness area in Canada that promised abundant wildlife and fabulous fishing.

"Hey how about this, it looks like fun?" I suggested.

Catherine hesitated, "That might be a little too much for me."

"Aw, come on. Did you see all those fish they were catching?" I asked in hopes of convincing her.

She countered with, "Yeah and the bears and those big moose

on the lake shorelines, and tents, sleeping in tents, drinking water from the same lakes that all these creatures do their… well you know."

"Don't you want to have the ultimate outdoor adventure?"

Her hesitation said it all, but then she surprised me with, "I guess we could try it."

The wild fishing, boating, camping, outdoor trip was billed as the trip of a lifetime, a most memorable experience, but it wasn't without risks. We did our research, contacted the outfitter, and made arrangements for what sounded like a primitive trip into the Canadian wilderness. Canoeing and camping in a huge area purported to be loaded with lots of fish swimming in *drinking water* lakes. The promise of abundant wildlife in the form of moose, bear, beaver, eagles, and of course the fish was a big draw. Catherine was very timid about the prospect of tent camping in bear country, and the thought of drinking water right out of the lake gave her frightening visions of various physical abnormalities. The talk of bears did little to convince her this was a good idea—maybe a tamer destination was more to her liking.

After a long plane ride from civilized St. Louis, then to Minneapolis, we boarded a puddle jumper joined by eight other passengers. We made our way to a tiny US border airport in International Falls that wasn't much more that a repurposed military Quonset hut. The flight attendant surprisingly reappeared as a luggage handler once we landed, and then there was the transportation offered—a heavily used van with faded paint and balding tires described in the travel brochures as a *limo*. Four hours after a border crossing into Canada and we were standing in the middle of a large log building going through our gear scattered out across a well-worn wooden floor—cookware, tents, sleeping bags, and food choices for the next five days.

The earlier fake smile Catherine bravely displayed was slowly disappearing as reality set in. I was conflicted as to whether to tease her with false frightening outdoor tales or to try to calm her with assurances that everything would be all right.

The outfitter, Bud, offered a look at the map of the general area we would be traveling, which closely resembled a maze of oddly shaped lakes, some so wild and so remote they were yet unnamed. The topography of the map showed rough terrain and was marked with red ink arrows indicating the most likely areas with the presence of bears. Bud's nonchalant description of what to do in case of a bear encounter did little to ease our concerns. "Bang pots together, yell, and make yourself look large," he advised.

I laughed; Catherine had long since lost her brave face.

The next morning, we were transported in four-wheel drive vehicles to a launch point, given brief, unclear instructions and bade farewell. In a canoe fully loaded with gear and grub, we made our way to the first portage area, which required us to unload and transport everything across rough land, uneven turf, soggy bottomland, fallen trees, and boulder rocks—all obstacles to the next navigable lake. Eventually we spotted a suitable camp site to make our *home* for the next several days.

My attempt to lighten the mood failed. "We'll take turns tonight being on bear watch."

"What?!" Catherine asked in a frightened tone.

"Just kidding. We'll be fine."

As we finished setting up camp, I started our cook fire and broke out the ham steaks designated as first night in supper and started cooking while swatting mosquitoes and watching the woods for intruders that might have winded our cook fire smoke. The sun was beginning to set, and the rising smoke trail showed the wind to be blowing from the west.

"So, what's with the can of peaches you had them put in our food pack?" wondered Catherine after the hastily prepared meal.

"When I came up with my father all those years ago, he had a can of peaches. As he ate them by the light of the campfire, I asked exactly the same question."

"And?"

I took a deep breath. "Well, here goes. I watched as my father struggled with one of those old hand can openers. With a little muttering and cussing, the can was open. He took a fork and began eating the contents. I watched as peach syrup dripped down his chin.

"I didn't know you like peaches," I said.

He looked up at me and said, "It's not the peaches, it's the memory."

"I don't get it, Dad?"

"Grandpa Vincent told me that Grandma loved peaches. Times were tough, and money was short, but as a special treat when he had a little extra money, he would bring her home some peaches, fresh if they were available, canned if not. During her sickness it was a little respite from the pain, and she enjoyed the extra special attention. He always liked the memory more than the peaches and occasionally he would slice fresh peaches from the backyard tree and put them in glass of wine."

I noticed my father was choking up while relating the story and quickly commented, "Wow, that's a great story."

Now Catherine was staring at me, and in a few minutes, I noticed her head nodded forward. She was trying to stay awake, but the nods and yawns gave her away."

"A little too much adventure for the day?" I asked, no answer, "Did you hear me?"

"I did, just sleepy," she responded with a deep yawn.

About then an unidentified, wild noise pierced the night air.

"What in the world was that?" was the anxious question Catherine posed.

"Probably a moose cruising the shoreline. It won't bother us. Besides, the bears will likely scare it away." I couldn't help but laugh.

Catherine stated the obvious, "There's no way I'll get any sleep tonight."

I suppose we've all had those nights when you want to go to sleep, tired but you just can't shut down for whatever reason. I know for me I'd be hoping for daylight, but it seemed that the clock had stopped. There's something about the early morning emergence of sunrise transitioning from the darkness and the arrival of each new day that is comforting.

"It's going to be fine. I thought you wanted to travel and have adventure?"

"This may be a little more of an adventure than I wanted."

After a long night filled with owl hoots, wolves howling, and assorted night noises, we awoke to the sound of the waves lapping onto the shoreline. Rising early, I built another fire using the embers from last night's cook fire, soon coffee—or a reasonable facsimile—was steaming from well worn metal cups.

"Are you excited to fish today?" I asked.

Her response, "Is it time to go home yet?"

Day one provided sunburned noses, sore backs, and more fish catches than should have been legal.

Each of the evenings brought conversations about the day's activities, but one element of vacation I recognized and enjoyed was the mental freedom that brings uninhibited thoughts.

Staring off into a campfire, I was transported to another time in my life. Maybe this trip was subconsciously an attempt to recapture a precious time in my life—my graduation trip with my father. I had his undivided attention. I saw him in a different light, not the well-dressed businessman, but there was an innocence to his apprehension about this environment, a different kind of rugged, a huge departure from his normal surroundings.

I watched as the wind carried a few campfire embers skyward and smiled at their imitation of what I saw as red lightning bugs dancing briefly then disappearing in the sky.

"You look like you're a thousand miles away," Catherine commented.

"We are, aren't we?"

"No, I mean, in another world or place in time."

Fighting the emotion, I responded, "I remember when I last visited this place with my father. Maybe that's what drew me here. He was so far out if his element, he unselfishly went into an uncomfortable situation just for me. That was brave and so kind of him."

Catherine just looked at me, and I knew she understood without verbalizing it. It was a tender moment in a not so tender environment.

The next few days delivered lots of fish, more sunburned faces, and the unmistakable personal aroma of campfire smoke, fish, and sweat.

Catherine suffered through the next three days and was more than glad to break camp and start to paddle the canoe back to civilization.

The journey back was quiet. Sometimes words aren't necessary. I was hoping it wasn't because she was disappointed. Maybe she was just taking in the view as we headed back from our adventure. This was an unforgettable memory, clean air, clean water, a world of wildlife, a full moon—good, bad or otherwise it was etched into our mental scrapbook.

Next up, Hawaii. I had been before, but Catherine hadn't. Using the benefit of my experience, I explained the Hawaiian language has only 13 letters, the beaches are beautiful, and do *not* eat the Poi. As the islands came into view from the airplane windows, the true beauty of this place for a first time visitor became evident in my travel partner's face.

For a week we took bus tours, visited the Dole pineapple plant, the Polynesian village, the Hawaiian zoo, and the eerie seaside memorial at Pearl Harbor—that was a sobering experience to stand on the platform above the sunken hull of the battleship Arizona. It was easy to imagine the chaos and historical and horrible significance of this sacred spot. There was a visitors' center with lots of artifacts, and most people walked in a silent reverence.

"This is a strangely interesting place," Catherine noted.

It took me moment to find my words." I agree, Catherine. I just imagine what this looked like and the carnage and tremendous loss of life in this very place."

We walked quietly, holding hands as a comfort to each other, pausing occasionally to look around and listen to others who expressed similar sentiments.

There's a certain charm to being on vacation.

"Tony, thanks for making this trip. I know you've been here before, and it makes you a great tour guide. I have to admit it's so relaxing not doing any cooking, cleaning, laundry, grocery shopping, or running errands. I don't even have to make the bed; this is like being in another world."

"It's fun for me because you seem fascinated by all the new experiences and almost become childlike."

She smiled at the comparison.

We baked ourselves on the beach, and we acted like typical tourists. The nights rekindled romance, and we found ourselves walking the beach after dark, again clutching hands and enjoying the foreign sights, sounds, and smell of the ocean.

"Let's get matching Hawaiian print shirts," Catherine suggested.

"You can't be serious," I replied.

"Why not?" she asked.

"Only if I can wear calf-high black socks with leather sandals, a plastic lei, and a little straw hat."

"You'd look ridiculous."

"Exactly my point."

Overwhelmed by the moment, Catherine looked at me and said, "This is what I dreamed about and imagined what travel would be like. I love it, and I love you."

"Aloha wau iā 'oe, that's I love you in Hawaiian. Don't ask me how to say anything else, it's all I know."

"I don't care, there's nothing else I'd want to hear." She smiled.

The Hawaii trip was more than checking a box off the bucket list, it seemed to relax us both and give us a peek at the possibilities of future travel plans. On the plane ride back, we were already thinking about the next destination. It sounded like another *non-fishing* trip. She voted for the Grand Canyon. I suggested a car trip across the wild west. We compromised, kind of. New Orleans it was.

We volleyed back and forth about the French Quarter, we booked a room at the Monteleone Hotel, the oldest hotel in the area with a reputation for fine food, the carousel bar, and world class hospitality. We were interested in the Cathedral of St. Louis—again the oldest in the area—the café du monde (which translates from French to "coffee of the world"), and all the activities on Bourbon Street. The cuisine and history were a draw, but the nightlife was of little to no interest—not to us.

Exuberant, Catherine asked as the airplane wheels screeched to a landing, "What should we do first?"

My reply, "I vote for a nap."

"No way, I want to see everything. We can sleep at home."

An easy flight and a cab ride to the hotel were both uneventful, but the cab ride to downtown New Orleans had us both peeking out the windows, and we agreed Bourbon Street did look like it could be wild even during the day.

Small shops, restaurants, strip joints gently described as *gentleman's clubs*, the ornate architecture of each building with wrought iron balconies, and the whole place seemed alive with activity.

I remarked, "It looks like an adult Disney World."

"Looks like a lot of fun to me," Catherine responded.

Her innocent side was always evident, and my habit of being constantly on guard was oblivious to her.

"I know you're fine, but I'd rather we stay together the whole time," I requested.

Then the famous words of all the trusting souls came out, "Oh, we'll be fine. What could happen?"

I avoided the response that would have shaken her to her core.

"Let's get unpacked and ask the concierge what the best things are to see, best places to eat, and what to avoid."

In the hotel lobby, a distinguished looking man in black formal wear was seated at a ornately carved wooden podium. "Excuse me sir, we're in town for few days. Could you make suggestions as to the best things to experience in the city and any cautionary advice?"

"My pleasure. For the full New Orleans experience, the obvious Café Du Monde, get a coffee and a beignet, take an outside seat and watch the passersby. You're a short walk from the St. Louis Cathedral, you'll see street performers, but stay alert for pick pockets and beggars—neither are violent, just pests. Don't miss out on the small shops and local foods."

I had already put my wallet in my front pants pocket and wrapped two large rubber bands around my wad of cash. Rubber bands make it hard to slide the cash out of the cloth pockets.

"How about Bourbon Street? "I inquired.

"Safe during the day, travel in group at night, and stay on the main drag."

"One last question, as far as food, who makes the best red beans and rice?"

"If you want the honest truth, the franchise Popeye's has the most authentic red beans and rice in all of Louisiana. Make sure to try a Cuban sandwich from one of the restaurants before you go home wherever that is," he said with a chuckle.

Typical tourists, as recommended our first day walking tour we went to get a beignet and coffee. Right after that we went inside the cathedral and marveled at the majesty of the high, beautifully painted ceilings, even our footsteps sound reverent as they echoed off the stone walls, and admittedly, we were entertained by all the street performers. There were musicians, mimes, and even young boys doing a sort of tap dance with bottle caps stuck to the bottom of their shoes.

At dusk we decided to brave the fabled French Quarter streets for supper and found a quaint Cajun café.

The menu displayed some strange fare; duck, crawfish, regular gumbo, okra, chicken-andouille gumbo, or other Creole dishes, strange names, and there it was, the Cuban sandwich, lots of meats that had been marinated in some concoction called *mojo sauce*, stacked on a crusty bun with a healthy (not heart healthy) portion of cheese. I was thankful that small stars to the left of the choices indicated the amount of heat to each dish. For me, description that ends in the word *pepper* is out.

"Okay, what are you having?" Catherine asked suspiciously.

"I'm going to brave the Cuban sandwich. How about you?"

"I've never had duck but there's a glazed duck on the menu. I'm going to try it."

"When the waiter showed up, I tried to impress him with my best local accent and pointed to the menu and proclaimed, "Cubano." Recognizing my out of town bogus accent, he smiled but said nothing. I figured this was to protect his post meal tip.

Catherine requested the glazed duck offering the side note, "I've never had duck before, I've heard it's greasy if not prepared correctly."

The waiter replied as if insulted, "No greasy duck here, madam."

We looked around and saw, much like us, the tourists were easily recognizable. New clothes, cameras strapped around the necks, that lost look, and nervous chatter.

We hurried through our meal so we could walk Bourbon Street and retire safely to our room before the evening's debauchery began.

Working our way through the streets, we saw lots of bizarre clothing options, many folks wearing beads, and we curiously noticed the local custom of people on the balconies throwing beads to the street bound on-lookers or scantily clad women, feather accents, heavy make-up, and strange hats were the uniform of the day apparently.

Catherine embraced all this travel with an unbridled enthusiasm. I, on the other hand, had been required to travel often for business purposes. Travel plans, arriving and departing schedules were viewed as mundane and subject to change for various reasons, most of which I had little or no control over.

Along the way I honed my travel skills which Catherine quietly observed until one day she asked, "What's up with the backpack? Why do you carry it?"

"After years on the road or in the air, I've encountered lots of surprises. Way before I met you, I tried to assemble a kit that covers most of the unforeseen eventualities. Airlines stopped serving meals, so for a while I made bacon sandwiches to take on the plane. Next was what I refer to as my necessaries, a spare cell phone charger, a small flashlight, a spare pen, notebook, an extra pair of underwear, a lightweight change of clothes, a bag of candy, a small towel, and a fifty dollar bill pinned to the inside of the backpack. Flight delays or cancellations, even being stranded in the airport are all very real possibilities."

I waited for a response. Instead I got that look that says, "Really?"

After the long pause, I offered, "More than once it saved me."

"Whatever you say dear."

Now I imparted some unrequested words of wisdom. "There are three kinds of people, those who make things happen, those who watch things happen, and those who say, "What happened?"

More travel and genuine adventure to come, buckle your seatbelt!

Chapter XVII

Changes and Challenges

I seemed there was the never-ending threat of *the curse*. According to the dream and story related to me, it was supposed to last one hundred years—if you believe in those sorts of things. Even though we were way past the hundred-year mark, it often appeared there was no escape.

I was truly a man in search of peace and harmony.

The troubling letters threatening Catherine came infrequently but remained a genuine concern. Then the number of letters increased. This cruel terrorism created a genuine concern, and the ugly truth is, evil people won't come after you—they go after what you love. I loved and cherished my Catherine.

The recurring thought so engrained in my head and replayed so often was my father's words, "Family is everything!" Was he right? Or was that an outdated concept that died with him and the old timers? Vince's horrific and untimely death pushed us all further apart. Now with both parents gone, the glue that kept us together had allowed jealousy and animosity to creep in. The competition for our parents' approval seemed to be a catalyst for discontent. Money was a false measure of success and did little to quiet the competitive chaos among the remaining family members. In the meantime there was life to live. Maybe there would eventually be a sort of reunion, I didn't even know if that were possible. Once any trust, even among family, is lost, could it ever be regained? It was my contention that those closest to you can hurt you the most. Sad.

In spite of all the past failed relationships, there were very few dark clouds hanging over Catherine and my heads.

"Do you ever see repairing the rifts between you and your siblings?"

Pondering the question, I looked at Catherine. "Why should I? I'm pretty happy with the way things are now."

"Don't you miss the bond of family?"

"I have that bond with you and our family," Was my response.

She pressed on, "What about the memories? What about the good times? Surely there were some pleasant times."

"Maybe in *your* childhood. Mine was riddled with being bullied by my own brothers just because they were older and bigger."

"They must have done something right."

"They did. They served as bad examples of what *not* to do. Vince's arrogance, poor judgement, and inability to keep quiet got him killed. Dominic—well, Dominic was the poster child for every other bad behavior. He thought my father and our last name gave him a pass card and shielded him from anything. Sorry I'm ranting, but I'm pretty passionate about the topic."

While I understood Catherine's desire paralleled mine for peace, sometimes it's better that things be left alone.

"How do you think your father would feel about the current state of family affairs?" Catherine pushed.

"I don't think that's a fair question. I don't want to be ugly about it, but I knew my father like very few people did. I tried to understand him on his own level. He grew up fast and hard, he knew the world didn't abide foolishness. Maybe I'll pay the price, but I, much like my father, am a major league grudge-holder, and it's gotten me this far. I think it's the purest form of survival instinct!"

"Pure? No. Even if you're right, look at the price you're paying, bitterness!"

Tired of the discussion, I tried to end it. "I'd really rather not talk about this any further."

The look on Catherine's face told me it would be a quiet, cold night in the bedroom.

I thought I had narrowed down where the threatening letters may be coming from. Now I believed my ex-wife, Carla, might have been the culprit. It was just a gut feel. Maybe it was someone I dated previously, maybe some silent stalker, or even the mysterious Amy. But Carla remained the prime suspect. Post-divorce she was bitter. She had envisioned and hinted at the hope of possibly a reconciliation. We saw each other casually just to settle any lingering business, When we did, before I prepared to leave, she always attempted to initiate a sexual encounter. I spurned every advance knowing it would just further cloud the waters and be disingenuous on my part. I didn't love her anymore.I began to recount the sum total of our relationship which started well and then sank to the darkest depths of avarice towards each other.

There were so many indicators, things as simple as a verbal sparring match which occurred in a shopping mall parking lot. On a routine trip to run necessary errands, Carla, who was always anxious to criticize, began a verbal critique of my driving.

In an angry loud voice she began, "This is a one-way lane!"

Recognizing an opportunity to return the volley I responded, "I'm only going one way." I smiled at my instantaneous witty come back only to invite the next verbal assault.

Now, with her volume up and face red, she attempted to one up me. "Don't you see the arrows?"

Not wanting to miss an additional chance to poke the bear, I blurted out, "I didn't even see the Indians."

So many unhappy memories.

Words became weapons. Toward the end, she said, "I can just walk away!'

I responded, "I'd hoped you'd run!"

It was over.

Eventually the nasty notes just stopped. A few months after that I got an email from my former brother-in-law informing me that Carla had died. That was completely unexpected, but mystery solved, back to normalcy—or so I thought. I realized that I really didn't know how to feel about this. I knew I didn't love her anymore, but the animosity had faded, and I didn't wish death upon her. It's been said the opposite of love isn't hate, it's indifference. I was in a different place in my life. I had someone who loved me, took care of me, and was everything that my ex-wife wasn't. I did feel some pangs of guilt over the nastiness that transpired between us during and after our marriage. It didn't know any specific details about her death and didn't want to know. But the concept of death still confounded me. How is it you're here and then just—gone?

News such as this sends me into a time travel of reviewing aspects of my past, how I treated people, should I have been kinder, more forgiving, or was I using my personal self-defense mechanism to keep from being hurt, vulnerable?

My fear of my short-lived hedonistic affair with Amy would resurface eventually was confirmed by a letter that stunned me and shocked me to my very core. It read:

It's time for clarity. Us meeting at Blue Springs State Park wasn't accidental. I took a page out of your Italian mob playbook and watched you for quite a while, noting your every move, studying your daily habits and rituals. I wanted you dead! You see, Mike Cooper was my father, and he worked for the F.B.I. for years. He disappeared when I was a young girl, and they never could find him or his body. Everyone suspected your father had him killed but just couldn't prove it. I grew up bitter never knowing much about my father, but I was surviving on a trust fund. I would have gladly done without the money to have my father in my life. I yearned for an opportunity to exact revenge. For a while your brother Dominic was my target. After stalking him I managed to introduce myself. He was easy, a sucker for a compliment and flirty conversation. I briefly dated him to draw him in close enough for my retribution. When he attempted to take me to bed it felt so wrong, just creepy. I couldn't figure out what brought those feelings on so intensely, but I ended any contact with him immediately and set my sights on you.

I was bitter. I had been deprived of doing normal father/daughter things. So I plotted my revenge. I devised an intricate plan to lure you literally into my web. My interest in entomology was peaked when I studied the black widow spider. The female, after mating kills her suitor—I admired that characteristic. Remember the black velvet choker with the single red glass bead, it was the mark of the female black widow, black with a single red marking! I could poison you with cyanide and make it look like a heart attack, get away, and nobody would be the wiser. That's the kind of vengeance I wanted, then I would feel relief from the torture of your family destroying my family. After our brief time together, I realized the death sentence I was going to impose on you would only parallel my own fate. You and your family would suffer the classic pain of paying for the sins of the father.

I couldn't bring myself to do it. I'm not by nature a religious person, but I knew enough to be aware of the Bible verse "Vengeance is Mine sayeth the Lord." That alone spared you. I decided to leave and go about my life. I'm still bitter about losing my father, no matter what the grudge was between your family and mine, but I'm seeking peace now, I hope you find your own peace.

Amy Cooper

Wow! My stomach was in knots. I'm sure all the blood had drained from my face—this plot was sick and twisted. I was nauseated and thankful that somehow, I had unknowingly cheated death. Then it struck me, I realized, this also meant that Amy was Dominic's half sister! This whole ill-advised tryste now took on a sort of overwhelming incestual feeling for me.

Another sickening aspect was that step-brother and step-sister had come dangerously close to intimacy.

Was this truly over?

Would this family ever be truly free of the curse?

Dom got married. His motivation was to use her for her savings, retiremen,t and insurance, and eventually, after he used her up, get divorced. This fit his abnormal behavior and didn't surprise me at all. My contempt for him pushed me to recall his empty pledge when he was in fear of his life, "I'll change, I promise."

I just added *liar* to his resume of *thief* and *bully*.

He ghosted me for years. That was okay with me, I had no interest in tracking him down.

Mary Rose, Dominic's co-conspirator eventually went broke. Her husband had enough and filed for divorce. This reaffirmed my belief in that eventually everyone gets what they deserve, good or bad. Karma? I'm not sure. I did wonder after hearing of her misfortune if she had genuine regret, or if that just regretted getting caught. Another cross for her to bear was that her kids abandoned her. She learned that there are often long-term consequences to ill-advised schemes. As her troubles piled up, I viewed her much as I saw others who chose alternative paths to life—there's a terrible price to pay, and once you hit rock bottom it should be a wakeup call, because after all, you can't fall off the floor.

I struggle with forgiveness but take the stance life will dole out its own punishments, and there's the ultimate price to pay in the eternity of the afterlife.

Word came to me from an old family friend that she had seen Mary Rose, and she had turned her life around. Enormous loss had sent her spiraling into a previously undiscovered darkness. She was living at a level of poverty previously unimaginable and unknown, certainly unfamiliar to her.

She was living in a one-bedroom apartment that was sparsely

furnished and just getting by on a small alimony allotment and a paycheck from a recently found job. This was a different world for her after her luxurious lifestyle funded by treachery and an honest, hard-working husband. Mary Rose finally had found her calling—she ran a home for wayward girls; troubled, addicted, or pregnant teens who needed a new start or a second chance were her clients.

I'm sure this was a bitter pill to swallow for the woman once consumed by images, real or imagined, of high society. Was this a turn around or a next level hidden agenda to reclaim her supposed *status*?

I was satisfied to leave things the way they were and not attempt to contact her.

Catherine questioned my motive. "Aren't you interest in the least in rekindling the relationship with your sister?"

"It's been this long, and I've gotten along fine without her. Why disturb the situation?"

"Yeah, but that's your sister," she insisted.

"She can be my sister but from a distance," was my rapid reply.

"That doesn't make sense," Catherine continued.

"What do I gain by having her back in my life?" I asked.

The speed with which I replied, and the increased volume of my voice was evident by the look on my wife's face.

Conversation over.

This is exactly why I abhor these interactions; somebody always gets their feelings hurt.

It seemed that people in my life, the ones who should have been closest to me just disappeared in a vapor. By now you'd think I'd get used to the unexpected surprises, the interruptions to my otherwise peaceful existence but...

A very unexpectedly letter arrived that would clear up one mystery and actually change what I believed. I opened the envelope, and there was a picture—to my complete and utter surprise it was Dominic and he was in a clerical robe that would be reserved for a man of the cloth.

"What?" I blurted out. "This can't be real!"

Curiosity peaked, Catherine asked, "What is it?"

"It's from Dominic."

In a high pitched voice, she asked, "Your brother Dominic?"

"There's a picture. He is standing on a white sand beach; I wonder if it's a Halloween outfit or a practical joke?"

A letter was also in the envelope, it's not often anymore that you get a real handwritten letter. The letter was short. I read skeptically, but the news was welcomed. It read:

> *Dear Tony, years ago I promised I would change. I know you didn't believe me, and I didn't blame you. I was ashamed of the person I was. I had tried women, booze, and drugs and decided it was time I tried God.*

I was in total shock, but this really does prove God moves in mysterious ways. My eyes teared up as I reread the letter twice and then just stared at the picture. He had gone to school to become an ordained minister and had relocated to Haiti to lead a church and devote his life to the poor. In my evening prayers I always included those closest to me and those who should have been closest to me. Although I know it's biblically mandated, I struggled with praying for my enemies.

After a few minutes I handed the picture and letter to Catherine as proof that I wasn't imagining this whole thing. Long ago I had given up on Dominic, but God hadn't. Hallelujah!

Chapter XVIII

Vacation or Vendetta

Quite unexpectedly a chance to combine travel with business and competition had arisen. There was a company in Rome, Italy, that was looking to hire me as a consultant to assist in improving their position internationally. Their requirements were things I was well versed in—I could sell and install my Supply Chain program to them and train their ownership and upper management in the use of the software. I would be responsible to educate them on the fundamentals and background theory behind the system. This was the perfect opportunity to mix business with pleasure and have Catherine accompany me. I was pretty sure she would jump at the chance for a European adventure. My expenses would be covered, and my compensation was the agreed to $2,000 dollars per day for the required amount of time and $25,000 for the software, and I still retained ownership.

"What would you say to a trip to Italy?"

She looked over the rims of her glasses. "Are you kidding?"

"No, ma'am! There's a large corporate firm in Rome that wants our computer business model for supply chain management. We can make it a business trip and a pleasure trip."

"How exciting!" She beamed at the thought.

"Business travel usually isn't very exciting. Long hours, grabbing meals when you can, endless meetings and lots of repeated questions."

A concerned Catherine asked, "What will I do while you're tied up with this project?"

"Are you kidding? There so much to see, you'll love it."

This business trip would require a change in mind set. I had very little patience for people who were indecisive. In spite of my long-time employment duties and the analyzing skills needed, once I left the corporate world, I migrated away from being a data gatherer, meeting attender and report analyzer. That was my business life. I had left it behind years ago. Now it was time to dust off my business persona.

While researching travel plans, I had learned of an international martial arts tournament scheduled at the same time as our trip and in of all places, Rome, Italy.

During my previous martial arts years, I had entered a few karate tournaments at the urging of my friends, students, and Mr. Williams. I surprised everyone, including myself, by winning first place in the fighting category for my age group. Over the next few years, I managed to do well, actually winning in different martial arts categories three years in a row in the fighting competition. Trophies displayed in a corner of my office were more a reminder of my midlife crisis to prove myself than as a challenge to continue.

While we were finalizing our plans, I casually mentioned this odd circumstance to Catherine. "What would you think of me competing in an international karate tournament while we were in Rome?"

A brief pause was followed by, "You're kidding, right?"

"No, it just happens to be perfect timing," I said.

"Perfect for what?"

"We'd already be there, and I could test myself against some strong competition," I proclaimed.

"What if you got hurt, then what?" the ever-cautious Catherine asked.

"What if I won?"

Coupled with an unmistakable look, she replied in *that* tone, "Sounds like your mind is already made up."

I sensed a softening to the idea. "Only if you're okay with it."

Then the dreaded words, "Do whatever you want."

Translation: *Go ahead and see what happens.*

No matter—I took it as a green light.

I hoped this travel and the freedom from routine would once again rekindle the fire and romance in our marriage.

Sometimes I had a flashback to the first night we made love, every detail etched forever in in my memory. It started out innocently enough, we were still kind of new to each other, Catherine was already at the house making supper when I came in, the scene was like one of the those made for TV romance movies.

After we ate, we stepped toward the large front window together. It was snowing pretty hard. I hugged her gently from behind, and she took my arms and wrapped them tighter around her.

I whispered in her ear, "That snow is really piling up now. I know this sounds forward, but would you like to just spend the night here instead of driving home?"

"Will you be a gentleman?"

"Of course."

"Well hell no, then I'm not staying."

I watched as she glided up the steps—she always moved like a ballerina, fluid, effortlessly, and graceful. I began to wonder what would happen next. Was this the night we made love for the first time? I feared rejection or damaging our budding relationship. My two biggest fears were failure and rejection, I could face both at the top of the stairs.

I was waiting nervously, sitting on the bed when I heard the shower stop, then the whirring noise of the blow dryer. After a few minutes the door opened, and I could see Catherine had raided my closet. She came out wearing one of my favorite shirts, old, soft from years of wear, a faded black-and-red checked flannel shirt. On her it looked like a night shirt. The room was dark other than a small light illuminating the room. She stepped out looking like a dream, an apparition floating toward me. After what probably was an audible gulp, I wondered again, *Was it time?*

All doubt was erased as she moved close and started unbuckling my belt. I was excited but nervous, I didn't take this lightly. Two people become almost like one, this is the ultimate gift, giving yourself to another person in a way that only you can give is sacred.

She stood in front of me and slowly unbuttoned each of the six buttons on the borrowed shirt seductively. "Is this okay?" she asked.

"It's more than okay." I felt my entire body tingle. Even my butterflies had goosebumps.

I kissed her on the forehead and on the side of neck—small, slow kisses.

"I just want to make you happy," I declared.

She responded, "Can we freeze time, you know, make time stand still?"

"Would that we could."

We spent the next hour exploring each other and making what could only be called sweet love, mixed with an unbridled passion I had never known before. At that moment we weren't aware that there was anyone else on the planet.

It was like a dream, an erotic dream, yet sacred. We were truly lost in each other.

We were for that time two bodies transformed into one, one soul, one heart, and forever changed.

Exhausted, I whispered to her, "To say I love you just doesn't seem like enough."

"I hope that's not just pillow talk. I love you; I feel safe with you."

"I've never felt closer to anyone than I do to you right now."

"Tony, I hope we can always feel this way. I admire your strength, and yet you can be tender, you're confident without being arrogant. I watch the way you treat people, it makes me love you that much more."

"I fall in love every day, but it's always the same, it's always with you. We're such a good team!"

A comment from Catherine, punctuated with a yawn, "I've also learned to trust you, that's big for me. I knew life could be good, I would have never imagined it could be this good."

Her eyes were closing, and the delivery of her words came slower.

Physically spent and totally satisfied, Catherine fell asleep with her head resting on my chest. Each time she exhaled I could feel the warmth of her breath as my chest hairs moved like tall grass in a breeze.

I prayed silently that I could keep this feeling forever, I wanted to stay right here, not have the sunrise anytime soon. I watched her sleep, she looked so peaceful, her hair reflected a radiant soft glow from the lamp on the nightstand.

She fell asleep, and I fell in love.

There were brief respites from our *adult time*. We attributed that to our ages, but we never lost that magic.

Arrangements made, plans in place, here we come, Italy! We both were excited, and better yet we were essentially traveling on somebody else's dime. Time for a transatlantic adventure.

Imagine, an offer from a large company whose primary interest was in exporting wine, cheese, and olive oil. They needed my expertise for setting up an international supply chain, and the pay was too good to turn down. And the worldwide karate tournament being held in Rome of all places—not exactly the location you imagine when you think of for a major martial arts event. Two opportunities to prove myself. This would be great, a work and play vacation! How fortuitous. Catherine was sold on the idea, at least the business and travel part.

Reservations were made, I had days, dates, and times to meet my potential business associates and filled out the necessary paperwork to compete in the karate tournament.

As we boarded the plane, we found out our seats were somehow separated—in a row of three seats, a lady was between Catherine and me. Thinking, *This isn't a good start,* I asked the human divider if it would be possible to switch seats.

"If I can have that window seat you've got a deal," she responded.

"Perfect. I'm Tony LeoMorte, and this is my wife, Catherine. We're headed to Italy... our first time."

"My name is Beth. This flight goes to Boston with a short layover and then I change planes for Rome."

"Same here, wow!"

"Business or pleasure?" she inquired.

I responded, "Oddly enoug,h both."

Catherine jumped in. "I'm so excited, I can't wait for the sites, the food, and shopping!"

"You're going to love it."

"So, Beth how about you? Have you been to Europe before?"

"Oh, several times, Honey. Make sure to visit the Coliseum, the Fountain of Trevi, the Vatican, and the open-air shops."

After an obscene amount of air travel in my lifetime, it was customary for me to just doze off, but Catherine was captivated by the view from 30,000 feet. Eyes closed, I could hear her and her newfound friend chatting about everything. Beth was a nature lover, hiker, collector of rocks, water color artist, and a teacher.

The next thing I remember was waking up to the sound of the skidding airplane tires as we landed, along with the announcement, "Welcome to Boston. If you have a connecting flight, there's a boarding information at the gate. The local time is 2:15 PM."

"Do I have time to visit the ladies' room?" Catherine asked.

"Of course."

A voice from behind us called out, "Wait for me, I'll go with you." It was Beth.

Guarding the carry-on luggage, I waited outside and had already figured out which direction our connecting gate was located.

"We don't have to hurry. We've got about an hour before we take off. Let's go to the gate and get checked in then relax," Beth the traveler proclaimed.

Gate 15 in the section for international flights had just a

few Italy-bound travelers already in line for boarding passes. At this point I was more concerned about our luggage being transferred. I could get new clothes, but my karate gear would be irreplaceable.

Beth's travel history was impressive—Italy, France, Germany, Ireland, and a few other places.

We soon found ourselves boarding for the transatlantic flight.

We would be flying over the ocean at night; a new experience for me. In about eight hours, if all went right, we would be touching down at Rome's airport.

After our arrival we gathered our luggage, and we exited to catch a ride to our hotel, the Hotel Italia.

As we were checking into the hotel, Catherine noticed a group of women standing together at the entrance to lounge/bar area. She looked at me and whispered, "I wonder if those women are waiting for someone?

Realizing her naivety, I leaned in to her and whispered, "Yes, they're all waiting for someone—they're waiting for their *dates*."

"How in the world could you know that?"

"I love you; you've led such a sheltered life," I replied with an audible chuckle. "They're what I refer to as, *soiled doves of negotiable affection*."

"They're what?" she called out.

I moved in even closer and whispered, "They're prostitutes."

"No!" she responded with a blush.

"Yes!"

Once in the room we decided to put on the tourist hat. We strolled past the open-air markets and found ourselves in the area of the Trevi Fountain.

Catherine spoke first, "Look at how clear and blue that water in the fountain is!"

The access to the fountain was limited, we waited to get close enough for the obligatory photo, and I suggested, "Let's put our feet in the water."

"You can't do that. It's actually illegal," Catherine advised. "I checked out everything about Rome."

"Okay, how about we work our way over to the Coliseum?"

"Let's go!" Catherine was excited to see all the sights.

After our arrival my personal tour guide started in. "I did research on the Coliseum; did you know it was started in the year 70 AD and would hold 50,000 to 80,000 people?"

"I'll remember that if I'm ever a contestant on *Jeopardy*," I replied.

"Wow, what a gift—international sarcasm," she said as she turned away.

"Sorry. I'm hungry, how about something to eat?" I asked.

As we cruised the area, we noted there were several choices.

"Oh look, there's a McDonalds," Catherine said, surprised.

I said, "You're kidding right?"

"No, I love the French fries."

"So, let me get this right, an Irish woman, married to Italian, in Rome, wants French fries?"

We wolfed down our first faux Italian meal and made our way back to the hotel. Catherine pushed the elevator button for the fourth floor, and as the door opened, we were surprised by how tiny this transportation device was.

Back in the room, I spotted a TV on a small table and switched it on. Hmmm…all the stations were speaking Italian and much faster than I could translate it.

"Hey, the towel racks are heated," came the sound from the next room.

I just smiled at my wife's childlike enthusiasm.

Opening a small closet, I immediately saw that there was a midnight black fleece robe with a bright red embroidered hotel insignia that read *Hotel Italia*. My mind raced to the thought that black and red color combination seemed inescapable and snapped me back to the eerie ribbon from my past dalliance.

I managed a call to my business associates and set up a time to meet them in the morning.

"We'll send a car to pick you up at 8 AM." Wow, this was first class treatment.

A nap, and then we were back on the historic streets of Rome. Hand in hand like young lovers, we walked lost in the atmosphere and architecture with the feeling of relationship renewal I'd hoped for.

Fearing jet lag and the time change might make me late, I asked the desk clerk for a wake-up call at 7 AM and as a backup set my phone alarm.

I was surprised at the small car sent to carry me to the world headquarters of Italo America Foods. Upon my arrival I was warmly greeted, and we got right down to business. I explained the intricacies of navigating international business and the importance of accurate forecasting of sales while staying aware of shelf life and the anticipation of delays. I brought up my computer model on a screen and explained in great detail the value of the program. They bought in!

After a brief discussion, followed by an explanation of terms and benefits, there was a formal contract signing. We agreed to meet again for two days to install the software and review expectations. That was easy!

On the ride back to the hotel, my mind turned to the karate tournament. I was registered and was nervous, probably more nervous than my primary reason for being in Italy, my consulting business.

Back in the room, Catherine asked, "So how did it go?"

"Smooth. It was easy and seamless. Now I can focus on the tournament."

"Are you worried?" she asked.

"Let's say apprehensive. You know me, I have that fear of failure. I've got tomorrow and then the tournament"

That evening I was probably bad company, focused on being mentally prepared to compete.

When Catherine woke up, I was in jogging clothes. "I'm going out and stretch and then run a little."

"Okay. When you get back can we get something to eat?"

"Sure, maybe we'll try one of the outside cafes."

The day passed as we took in the several walking distance local attractions. I was weary while Catherine was energized.

I asked Catherine, "Are you interested in coming to the karate tournament?"

"I don't think I can. If something happened to you, I don't know what I would do."

"I understand. It would probably make me more nervous if you were there anyway."

The morning of the competition we prayed together—it was our normal habit to pray before meals, at night and before we fished.Catherine had planned on sightseeing with her new friend Beth.

As I prepared to leave, I spent a few minutes just staring at my black belt and thought about all the work that went into achieving it. I thought of all those who came before me and traveled that martial arts journey—so many stories behind the belt. A lesson I struggled with at times is the center of true self defense, the goal if possible is the peaceful, non-violent resolution to conflict.

The previous night I arranged for an Uber-type ride to get me to the tournament. That morning another of the small Italian cars wound through the narrow Roman streets towards a modern-looking building nestled among the ancient structures that were typical of Rome.

Upon arrival I could tell this was someplace special, it was buzzing with activity, and I could sense excitement when I walked in. The walls were covered with flags from conceivably every country in the world. At the registration table, I was given instruction as to where to change and to the place serving as a warm up area and then competition location.

My competitor number was 22, my lucky number. My first match was in 45 minutes. The tournament was set up for the *kumite* (fighting) as a typical tournament—you fight until you lose—and I was entered in the age fifty-and-over black belt division. You compete to three points or until one person can't continue.

My initial match was against another American. Before the start a two-inch-wide red ribbon was tucked in the backside of my belt so the judges could identify me. And once again the black/red color scheme seemed to be a never-ending reminder of a dark circumstance in my life.

I scored quickly with a roundhouse kick to the head, my signature move. It makes your opponent look for the same attack which opens up punches to the body. He followed with a punch to the left of my head and then two more quick points for me, and I won the first match. Could I win the whole thing?

My next match was against a German in his mid-fifties, at least 10 years younger than me. At the start he came with a full force punch to my face which is frowned upon by the officials. *Okay, my turn.* They started us again, and I used a spinning heel kick to the liver. When properly executed, it's devasting. He went down and laid there until he was helped off the mat, signaling he'd had enough.

Thirty minutes later I was standing across from a Japanese man that truly had the look of a warrior. Any dreams I had of winning were gone as he quickly disposed of me with three straight points. I was proud of myself for competing and left with a medal and a memory.

When I arrived back at the hotel, Catherine was bubbling over.

"What are you so excited about?" I wondered.

"I'm just happy you came back vertical!" Catherine laughed. "And guess what?"

"I'm too tired to guess. What?"

Catherine excitedly announced, "Beth is continuing on to Ireland and has agreed to guide us if we want to go, she's been there before. We don't have to be back at any certain day, your business deal is done, we have lots of time—so, what do you think?"

"I say… yes!"

In a childlike voice came the simple response, "Oh goody!"
Ireland, adventure awaits.

Chapter XIX

Luck of the Irish

Years ago, we toyed with the idea of a visit to Ireland. I was in my father's old office, Catherine in the kitchen, she poked her head around the corner and asked, "You know I was wondering; we have more time now and the money, is there anything you'd like to do?"

"Yeah, maybe travel, take a vacation."

"Where?"

"Ireland, maybe Dublin, Ireland," I said with evil intentions.

At that time, I was wanting to avenge the death of my older brother, Vince, the namesake of Grandpa Vincent. He had been mistaken for being the father of the illegitimate child of Bonnie Dempsey, and her husband, Sean, blamed Vincent thinking he had been responsible. There was always bad blood between them after an incident at the restaurant where Vince was guilty of flirting with Bonnie in front of the jealous Sean. He later killed my brother and then ran like a coward, hiding out in his native Ireland. My mother never was the same, and my father was also a changed man for the rest of his days.

The last time I saw Bonnie, who my father affectionately called *Bunny* because of her Irish brogue, she hadn't heard from Sean for quite a few years. She did know he was hiding out in Ireland and had continued his carpentry work, but that was about it.

When I pressed her for more information, she said, "He had relatives living in Dublin, that's where he would most likely go."

Always wanting to know as much as possible about my

enemies, I continued, "What else about him? Any habits? Anything that you might remember."

"He has a habit of drinking daily, Irish whiskey and beer mostly. Oh, and he always carried a carpet knife in his pocket, wooden handle, hooked blade. That's probably what he used to kill your brother, Vince."

Secretly I never thought the opportunity would present itself to find him, but now—who knew? The fire of retribution burned in me.

With little effort we discovered that Rome to Dublin was a three hour flight and most reasonable in price.

Catherine did a little online research, the name *Dublin* comes from an Old Irish Gaelic phrase *Dubh linn* that translates to *Black Pool*. "Also, Dublin is crowded, it holds one-third of the country's population," she informed me.

Black, of course, more of the dark side.

Beth told us she had a few friends living in the city. One in particular was a longtime resident named Ansley.

Secretly I questioned her, "Beth, how well do you know this woman, Ansley?"

"I've known her for more than 10 years."

"Do you trust her, trust her judgment?"

"I do."

"I'd like to look up an old acquaintance. Maybe she can help me track him down?" I asked innocently.

Beth confidently responded, "If she can't help, she'll know somebody who can."

"After we land and get settled in, see if you can get a hold of her please."

Catherine sat quietly, deeply entrenched in a travel magazine, not hearing the hushed conversation.

I didn't want to tip my hand, because I knew what would happen. She would never agree to go. Most surely, she would be on the next flight to the United States had she known the real reason for my interest in Dublin, Ireland.

Once we arrived Beth went right into action and contacted Ansley. Catherine was anxious to tour Dublin and check out the shopping, see the sites, and try new foods. She waited in the room, while I started my trip to the dark side.

Next, an exploratory phone call. Without giving away my intentions I planned to seek details and asked about the area and its residents. "Ansley this is a friend of Beth's, Tony LeoMorte."

"Hello, I really like your name!"

"Thanks, I got it for my birthday," I snapped back.

"Oh, an American sense of humor, I like that."

"I was wondering, do you know a lot of people in Dublin?"

"Certainly not everyone but a bunch of them. My family has been here for generations. If I don't know the people, they know us, but there are a lot of people living in Dublin. I'm pretty sure we can find your friend."

My friend, I thought. *Hardly my friend.*

"What can you tell me about him?" she asked.

Not wanting to tip my hand, I started slowly, "His name is Sean Dempsey. He does carpentry work, has probably been here for the last 25 years, and has family here."

She laughed, "Are you kidding mate, you couldn't swing a dead cat anywhere in Dublin and not hit a Dempsey."

"He likes to drink—Irish whiskey and beer."

Again, she tried to hold back her laugh. "That narrows it down to about 50,000 people. Is your friend a bit of a rogue?"

"You might say that," I answered.

"A good place to start then would be the Temple Bar District. It's a bit rowdy," she advised.

"Can you take me there and let me check it out?"

"Are you sure, mate? It might get a little rough for a out of town visitor," she voiced her concern.

"Positive." I replied.

"Okay, since your Beth's friend, we'll give it go. You've got my number, give me a jingle when you're ready."

In situations like this I always plan on utilizing all my experience to anticipate what might happen and am prepared with a plan of action. I also had the element of surprise on my side, a decided advantage for what I had in mind. I did wonder, though, what my father would have thought and what advice he might have given me.

I barely had any memory of what Sean Dempsey looked like, and it had been decades. I still believed I would recognize him. I also knew I was a stranger in this land, and regardless of what I did, even if my look didn't give me away, my voice, accent, and words would. I went as far as to exchange my paper bills for some local currency, the Euro, as to not draw additional attention by flashing United States cash.

I thanked Beth, then told Catherine, "I'm going to check downtown Dublin out; I don't think it's the kind of tour you'd be interested in."

A concerned Catherine asked, "Are you sure?"

I came back with, "Yeah, you and Beth can go do girl stuff."

"Do you think it's safe?" Catherine worried.

"You know me, I'm always careful. We'll do some tourist things together tomorrow." I immediately felt guilty for my omission of the truth, but I was determined to settle the score.

I made arrangement to meet Ansley outside our hotel at seven that evening. I described myself, and before I left the room put a bar of soap in a sock, tied a knot in it and tucked it into my back pocket. Some of our family associates used this set up like the old time, poor man's black jack. Nothing illegal about a bar of soap in a sock, but when someone is hit in the head with one swing, they normally would be knocked out.

Ansley was a typical Irish woman, red hair, short, looked athletically muscular, and she moved with purpose. She had a green four-leaf clover tattoo on the back of her right hand.

I thought, *How blatantly bold.*

After meeting Ansley, our first stop was the Lucky Leprechaun Pub. Just as I feared my looks, clothing and demeanor immediately gave me away, and I was approached by one of the local tough guys.

"What is this, mate, the American invasion?"

"Nope, just looking for a drink and a good time," I responded in a loud voice.

The local spokesman decided to have some fun at my expense, and in a loud tone said, "Maybe you should drink some milk, it's good for your teeth." With that his friends roared with laughter.

As to be sure to be heard above the crowd, I responded even louder, "You know what else is good for your teeth, mate? Minding your own business!"

A hush fell over the room, a pause, and then an explosion of more laughter signaled their drunken approval.

We slowly backed out of the bar, and headed for the next destination.

"You were right, Ansley, tough crowd."

"I've got hand it to you mate, you handled that well!"

We popped in and out of another half dozen dives, each looking like a back street bar from inner city St. Louis—smelly, crowded, and each had the look of a place where a brawl could break out at any moment. I moved cautiously and made myself familiar with where each exit was located.

Ansley pointed to another spot just across the street. "This next place may be where your friend hangs out. It's frequented by a lot of the local construction workers."

We walked to the next sleazy joint, the old wooden sign outside read, The Dew Drop Inn. It was the kind of place that looked like at the end of the night they had to mop up the blood and sweep teeth off the floor.

Smoke filled the air, and the smell was terrible, reeking of stale liquor and sweaty people.

My eyes slowly surveyed the room table by table, and there at the end of the bar sat a lone figure. It was him! He had not aged well, his face and body showed that life hadn't been kind to him. I figured there was no way he wouldn't recognize me. I suggested that Ansley wait outside for her own safety.

"Are you sure?"

"Absolutely. I've got this. I'm in my element."

I studied my intended target. He looked in my direction, paused and then went back to his beer.

I had two hypodermic needles, one in my jacket pocket and another in my right front pants pocket. Any drug store carries them. I had removed the caps and filled them with industrial drain cleaner I found in the closet of the first floor restroom of the hotel.

I knew regardless of my training and the hate I felt that would fuel me in my quest for revenge, Sean Dempsey had the home field advantage.

This is the guy that had unleashed unspeakable anguish on my family. I looked at a gaunt figure, hair matted and an uneven line across the back of his head like he attempted to give himself a haircut. His face weathered and covered with a six-day stubble, his eyes were hollow and sunk into the sockets. His clothes told another story, a story of hard living and being tattered and bounced around. Sean Dempsey humped over, alone. He had the look of a man who had spent decades living in his own personal prison.

I eased up behind him, still not 100% sure if it were him.

"Hello Sean. Don't turn around."

In a feeble voice he said, "Who is it?"

"Don't you remember me? We met in St. Louis several years ago, and I've traveled almost 4,000 miles to find you."

"No, I don't remember you. Why travel so far to find me?"

"Because I'm going to kill you. I just haven't decided how," I whispered in his ear.

"Kill me? Why?" he implored.

"My name is Tony LeoMorte. Do you remember now? You killed my brother Vince for no reason."

Now I could hear the fear in his voice.

"Please, no! You don't know how much I've already suffered. I was young, jealous, stupid."

This place was perfect—no surveillance cameras, boisterous crowd, and non-stop loud music. All I'd have to do is pull the cap off the needle, insert it at the base of Dempsey's skull and deliver the poison, quick and quiet.

He cried as he spoke now. "I found out that it wasn't your brother who betrayed me, it was my wife and that priest. Please, please. I'm just an old man, a broken old man. I'm begging you."

Enraged I spoke again directly into his ear, "You caused my family enormous pain, my mother and father suffered in anguish for the rest of their lives because of you. Do you think your tears can cheat me out of the satisfaction of my revenge?"

"Revenge? I've lived a tortured existence ever since I left, decades of remorse. Death might be easier than living this life, but again I'm begging you, let me live. I'm afraid to die."

I was infuriated and somehow conflicted by the words of this piece of trash murderer. The music almost drowned out my reply, "Why should I let you live?"

"Killing me won't bring back your brother, and if you're a man of faith, you'll understand. I've dedicated myself to atoning for my sin and found God. Have mercy on me, give me the same forgiveness I ask for daily from God. If nothing else does the Bible verse *Vengeance is Mine* mean anything to you?"

I stepped back and took a long look at this pathetic figure who was more in need of pity than in punishment. Then like a thunderbolt it hit me, when I was vulnerable and Amy Cooper had sworn revenge on me because my family destroyed her family, she couldn't bring herself to harm me. She reconsidered for the same reason quoting exactly the same verse.

I eased away, I stepped from the darkness of this dimly lit place into the bright street light outside and felt a burden had been lifted from me.

I recalled a verse, one of the beatitudes, *Blessed are the merciful, for they shall obtain mercy.*

I can't fully explain it, but I walked out a different person that when I walked in.

Time to go home.

Chapter XX

My Inheritance

In our world when you hear the word inheritance most likely you always think of money. It's true that money is important. I've been both poor and financially well off—I prefer the later.

It was well into the night, Catherine and I were lying in bed and neither of us was sleepy. This was the best time to have in depth conversations. I like substance, another session of pillow talk, when it's quiet, the day is done, and we can give each other full attention.

Out of the blue, Catherine said, "You think so much differently than anyone I've ever known. I often wonder how your mind works?"

After a pause I responded, "Part of it is an illusion. People have remarked about how smart I am, but I just have a great memory and solid vocabulary. That doesn't make me smart."

She countered with, "It's not just that. You see things others don't."

"It was both a blessing and a curse, I had to grow up fast, not by choice but necessity," I replied.

"Okay, what's your earliest memory?"

"You're going to think this is crazy, but I couldn't have been more than two or maybe three, but I remember laying on my back and seeing through the wooden bars on my crib the blooms on a mimosa tree waving in the breeze. I was on the second floor of the house; the breeze moved the sheer white drapes, and there were birds singing."

"And you remember that?"

"I do. I think I learn different than others and retain by repetition. Once I've got it, it's locked in. It's been both a blessing and a curse."

A large and most treasured part of my inheritance was the things I learned from my father and lessons from life. It seemed my father had a saying for every situation. I remember him telling me, "Hard work won't hurt you."

"I also remember the look of disgust on his face when I replied, "Maybe not but I'm not taking any chances."

She continued, with a yawn, "I watch you as you watch everything around you."

"Being observant teaches you a lot. I realized as you age mistakes get bigger and are harder to correct. I had lots of bad examples, and I promised myself to remember, you don't have to live it to learn it."

"I'm getting sleepy."

"Oh no, you started this; we're just getting to the good parts," I teased.

Another gem from my father was, "Never lie to anyone who trusts you, and never trust anyone who lies to you." I did eventually learn that people who lie to you about little things will most likely lie to you about big things. After many years I still wondered why people lie.

"I've become adept at picking up on people lying to me. Unfortunately, I had a lot of practice. I remember sitting next to my father and him telling the story to a man about his friend and true father figure, Tommy Russo. The story was when a protégé was getting a little too cocky. Mr. Russo brought him back to reality with the statement, "I taught you everything you know, but not everything I know." That stuck with me too."

Catherine pressed for more insight, "Do you think your father worried about things?"

"I think my father knew what to worry about and when to worry about it. He had a sixth sense. He knew with the money and power came a great deal of responsibility and that there were people who were jealous of his accomplishments. He once told somebody who questioned his rise to success, *the man at the top didn't fall there."*

I offered more, "I watch people, I want to know their motivation and intent. Men especially are motivated by three things, "sesso, denaro e potere."

An impatient Catherine asked, "In English please?"

My response, "sex, money, and power."

"I listen to what people say, and I listen closely when they're mad, they'll tell you all you need to know. I'm sure of this, my best lessons hardly ever came from a school room."

"Hardest lesson, what was it?"

"That's difficult to narrow down. One of the most difficult was the last few months of my first marriage. I sometimes laid there next to her and realized I really didn't even know who she truly was. I loved and her and trusted her, and she used that trust against me. Probably next, at least for me, was how fragile life is. You're here, you're gone. That taught me to value my time, use it wisely, and don't give it to things or people who aren't worthy of it."

After thinking about it, my inquisitive wife came back with, "Yeah, we really never know how much time we have."

"Here's another Big Tony true story—we're at the hospital visiting a friend of his who went by Chicago Mike. So, another friend of Mike's comes in to visit, and they're discussing his prognosis. Now Chicago Mike is a tough as a two-dollar steak, and after hearing Mike tell this guy about his condition, the guy asks, "So how much runway you think you have left?"

"Runway?" Catherine askes with a puzzled look on her face.

"Yeah, like before your number comes up. You're off to the see the Big Guy in the sky."

"And once again, in English please!" One of her favorite phrases.

"How much time you have left before you die," I say with a wry smile on my face.

I glance over at the clock on the nightstand, the red block numbers are indicating 11:48. Now I'm on a roll, but in two minutes she'll be snoring. This calls for an increase in volume. "I recall more advice my father gave Vincent, "You can think what you want, but be careful what you say." Too bad Vincent didn't heed those words, it likely cost him his life."

"This is about that whole Bonnie Dempsey mess isn't it?" Catherine asked with a yawn.

"Yes," I said in hushed tones.

With a little more conviction, Catherine said, "That woman is bad news. She almost destroyed our lives. It's bad enough what she did to your family already."

"Thankfully, that's over now. We're here, and we've got the rest of our lives together."

"That'll be a secret that no one else will ever know about."

I couldn't resist. "An old school belief that my father passed down was, *it's not a secret if two people know it.*" I continued. "The old time Italians had a saying; *the walls have ears.*"

"Really? Do you have any secrets?"

"Don't we all? And what about you? What lessons had the most impact on you?"

"It's late. I don't want to play anymore?"

It was lights out, but now my brain was in overdrive. I could feel the warmth of her body pressed against mine as we did the customary spooning. She dozed off, but I knew this would not be a good sleep night for me. Then again, I rarely experienced a peaceful sleep. Maybe it was the overwhelming feeling of responsibility for everyone in my life. I felt it was my job to keep my family safe and comfortable. I especially looked on the innocence of all the children as a dual responsibility, a blessing and a huge concern for ensuring their well-being. The times that we were all together were the best; I could watch over everyone, and I found an enormous peace at seeing them all sleeping—it was like Christmas each time.

The years had in a sense hardened me. It had turned into a

tough world out there, and all my real family needed me whether they realized it or not. The Bible and my world taught me the highest form of love you could offer was the willingness to give your life for those you loved. I was willing.

Maybe one day all of my family would understand these things, and that would be their inheritance.

Chapter XXI

So, This is How It Feels to Die?

Suddenly there were sharp pains in my chest. Previously I had ignored the dizzy spells, the blurry vision, and the pain running down my arm. Typical man, I played off anything being wrong. I had kept up with my regular checkups, changed my diet, no smoking, no drinking, and a regiment of regular exercise. I remember feeling light-headed and trying to speak, but I was merely mouthing words.

"I'm going to the bedroom to lay down."

The next thing I knew was hearing a frightened Catherine speak with an unusual tone in her voice, "Tony what's wrong?"

I knew what I wanted to say, but the words wouldn't come out. "I don't know."

"What should I do, call 911?"

I just remember the room spinning, and then the craziest thing was my vision went from pitch black to the brightest light I had ever seen. *Blinded by the light.*

I could still hear Catherine's agonizing words, "Operator send an ambulance, *please!*"

I could hear things going on around me, but I was plunged back into the dark.

In a few minutes, through my darkness, I could hear, "There's no pulse and no heartbeat."

A sense of calm came over me. There was no more pain. Light came slowly, and now I could just barely see through a sort of vapor. After a few seconds I could make out a figure in the distance moving toward me. It was Grandpa Vincent—he was wearing his old khaki pants, a white T-shirt, and his brown work shoes. It was the first time I had ever seen a big smile on his face.

Just over his shoulder... was it? It was. Grandma Rosa! She died over twenty years before I was born. She looked just like the only black and white family picture that I'd seen; it was glued into a family photo album; her eyes looked like two pieces of coal but with an unmistakable light somehow emanating from them. Her black hair pulled tight to her head; she was in a modest dress that hung to the floor. Imagine, I'm meeting her for the first time.

Next, I could smell him before I saw him, my father, Big Tony. I had saved his last bottle of after shave lotion and would unscrew the cap off the dark green bottle just to smell it when I missed him most. Sometimes I'd sneak into my office and wear his old hat to feel closer to him. It had a sweat stain ring, but his smell had long since disappeared. There he was, exactly how remembered him.

And my mother, Maria. I reached for her hand but couldn't find it. She was wearing her favorite dress, the rose-colored one, and she had that look of love only a mother could give.

Vince trailed behind; I'd forgotten what he looked like.

They all had the most welcoming smiles on the faces. There was no sadness, I was overjoyed to see everyone!

In the distance I could even see all our German Shepherds. One by one they ran up, tail wagging, and stopped a few feet away—except Samurai. As was her custom she came up on my left side and sat down. I reached down to rub her favorite spot between her ears, but I couldn't feel her.

One by one many more people from the past emerged through the mist; familiar faces I hadn't seen or in some cases thought about for quite a while.

Then in a deeply resonating but pastoral voice I heard this Bible verse, "He has delivered us from the power of darkness."

The joyousness of the reunion faded away as I slowly, oh so

slowly saw a dim light. I could barely make out a face. Then I heard Catherine's voice.

"Wake up Tony. That must have been some dream!"

About the Author

Joey Monteleone writes from his lake home on the shores of Woods Reservoir in Decherd, Tennessee.

Joey has for decades, been a media personality hosting a radio spot on WSM 650 as the outdoor editor of *Wild Side Radio*. He has appeared on TV and in person as a seminar speaker for over 35 years. Monteleone's outdoor writing career spans over 45 years, and he's a three-time Eastern United States karate tournament champion.

Joey and his wife, Debbie, fish over 100 days a year, and Joey holds the lake record on Woods Reservoir for largemouth bass, a fish weighing in at over twelve pounds. Previous published books include: *I'll Be Tennessean Ya', 60 Seasons, Secret of the Storms Cent Anni, Strictly BIG Bass*, and now the sequel, *Delivered From the Darkness – Cent'Anni book two*.